Notches

M. Ennenbach

Notches
Copyright © 2019 by M. Ennenbach
All rights reserved.

ISBN: 9781639510306

Published by Death's Head Press,
an imprint of Dead Sky Publishing, LLC
Miami Beach, Florida

www.deadskypublishing.com

Cover Art: Don Noble

To Maia Danae and Dante Xavier, no matter what happens in this crazy world, you two will always be what I am most proud of. I love you both to the Moon and back, always.

A special thanks to PC3 and Jarod for giving a chance to a strange writer that doesn't quite fit the mold. There aren't words of gratitude enough.

Contents

BLUE

My Dearest,

I hope this letter finds you doing well. I've found myself struck in a morose languish. I hope writing to you will release it's hold upon me incrementally as I've become unable to muster the energy to step outside this accursed hotel room. I fear the maids believe I've expired as the do not disturb sign has hung from the door knob for a week straight.

I miss the sound of the waves crashing and your singing as you sit in front of the fire. Miss the steady clack of your needles as you knit yet another masterpiece to keep us warm in the winter. I miss the touch of your hand upon my shoulder and crooked smile informing me to put my book down and come to bed. This distance is too great between us and I was meant for staying closer to home. My constitution demands the satisfaction of your lips upon mine. These Appalachian winds carry sickness and fear. I can't stand another breath of them. If they don't send me home to you soon I fear madness will quite overtake my brain.

And the dreams this place gives. A pox upon the mountain breeze and rambling wildlife. The sounds at night are quite enough to make the spine grow weak and the mind dip deeply into insanity. I know you are rolling your eyes at me as you read this. Thinking I've only caught a case of the over dramatic. You may be right. But be it the untamed wilderness or the lack of you by my side, these dreams take root and I cannot cast them out.

It isn't just me plagued by the accursed things. Why just this morning as we sat drinking coffee and dining on eggs and bacon and toast, Jeffrey confided in me that his sleep has become a tangle of dark portents. I tried to laugh it off but inside I felt the cold steel of terror as he described the very same images I have been haunted by. The room grew quiet as he spoke and I could see the uncomfortable faces of others that had suffered the same visions. None were willing to say anything. But I could see it as clearly as the clouds in the sky.

I was asleep. Dead asleep. No. Strike that. Soundly asleep. Better. I was dreaming. Not the recurring dream I told you about when I wrote to you last week. The one where you and I picnic down by the bay. The gulls crying and the gentle curve of your neck so intoxicating in the afternoon sun.

No.

I was sound asleep when I heard a tapping on my window. Being in the third story of the lodge my sleeping brain rationalized it as a branch against the pane. My cranky frame stretched up to open the window and trim the offending twig. But as I opened the curtains I saw no wind swept limb. I saw a girl. No more than thirteen or so. And she was standing outside my window tapping upon it with a small finger.

When she saw me staring back at her she smiled a smile that carried the warmth of the northern wind in mid-January. It chilled me to the bone to see this mockery of a smile. And I squinted my eyes to better make her out. She was no little girl, this I swear my love. Perhaps once she had been but no longer. Her skin was stretched too tightly across her skull and had a faint blue tint to it. Her lips were so dark they could have been black. And those teeth. Oh the teeth in her mouth had been filed to sharp points like a shark or tiger or some predatory creature meant for one thing. Killing.

And she stared at me with that smile that promised blood not joy and kept tapping the window. I stumbled back from the window and she began to moan, a sharp keening sound that felt like rusty nails down the back of my brain. I let the curtains fall closed and scurried back into bed. And a small laugh, filled with menace and promises of pain filtered through the glass and fabric.

I woke with a start and made my way hesitantly towards the window. And as I nervously peered out I let a soft chuckle as nothing but the treetops and moon greeted me. My heart still hammered in my chest as I lay back down and slept molested by dreams until morning.

You probably think it was the result of too much brandy by the fireplace. From smoking my pipe and imbibing with the others while sharing tall tales of the road. And I would tend to agree, you have a knack for seeing right through me like that. But then at breakfast Jeffrey told of the same evil little minion in his dream as well! Down to the smallest detail. We nervously laughed it off and he burned crimson as he realized how silly he must have sounded. But I tell you the laughter rang hollow out of my throat. Hollow indeed.

So now I sit with shaking hand on quill, excuse the spattering of ink on the page. We can call it the chills of an early winter. Yes. Let's do that. Not the baseless horror I felt last night and again at breakfast. But the onset of winter in a drafty lodge in the middle of nowhere.

Know my every thought is upon you my love as we brave another week or two in this desolate place. The surveyors sent word that they have narrowed down the richest three veins for mining and once they've finished we can set our minds to laying out the plans. Then I can catch the train back to you. Where I belong. I believe this will be my last job for the company. I know

I say that each and every time I head out but this time I mean it. I'm so very tired of the road and being away from you.

I will write to you in a few days my love. Hopefully with news of my return.

Love eternally

H. September the 20th, 1878

My Dearest,

Good day my love. Forgive the lateness in this letter. I had meant to write days ago but we found ourselves in the midst of crisis, one after another and time got away from me. I hate this damnedable place, truly a blight in this great nation. The natural beauty hides an undercurrent of pure evil, I swear this.

In my last letter I detailed that we were just awaiting word from the surveyors. After days of silence we decided to send a party out to find them and see what the hold up was. A band of the best trackers and hunters in the region, which says something as this land is as untamed as in the heart of Africa for sure. Filled with all manners of beast and men gone feral from lack of civilization. This is the land our grandfathers and great-grandfathers first landed upon after having left the only homes they ever knew in search of freedom and riches.

The search party sends back regular missives to let us know their progress and so far after days they have very little to report. It is as if the forests and mountains opened up and swallowed the surveying crews whole. Old campfires, weeks old they say, are the only sign they ever existed. We know the direction they were headed towards. But if they ever made it, there is trace to be seen.

The locals remain suspiciously hushed about it. Superstitious folk, the lot of them. They just make the sign of the cross and hurry off when we ask questions about the woods and mountains. It is infuriating to say the least. So we sit doing nothing while awaiting word on the missing men. Any more delays I doubt I will make it to a city to catch the train home this year. The air smells thick with snow and the clouds are heavy and block the sun on most days. But I keep optimistic as it is too easy to slip into a malaise up here.

On the dream front, since I wrote to you the dreams have all but stopped. Now my sleeping head is back to being filled with thoughts of you and I frolicking in the waves and laughing and loving. I fear it was the stress of the situation and cabin fever combined.

In fact, spirits overall are much improved besides the worry about the lost crew. But we all believe they will turn up soon enough. It isn't the first time a crew has gotten turned around in the dense trees and winding creeks up here. The lack of stars and sun to guide them probably has them hunkered down waiting for the right chance to make it back. Our meals are back to being filled with laughter and lies told for the sale of bigger laughter. An ever escalating event of frivolity from men desperate to be home but willing to brave it out a while longer.

All except poor Jeffrey. The fool ended up cracking open his window during the night a few days past. Now he is suffering from sickness brought on by the chill air in his lungs. The doctors claim he has no signs of illness, just lethargy as far they see. He mostly sleeps and drinks heavily of the tincture they make locally. A rather strong concoction capable of taking down a bear as the locals tell it. I took a drink of it and slept peacefully for nearly twelve hours. So I'll testify to its strength. But don't fear for Jeffrey, he'll pull through this. And possibly learn to leave the window shut during the cold nights.

I must go my love. I see the wagon pulling near the lodge and hope to hear good news. I shall write sooner, I swear. Until then know I think of you always and long to feel your lips upon mine.

Love eternally

H. September the 28th, 1878

My Dearest,

The last couple days have been fraught with ups and downs. I feel torn in multiple directions. As always I hope this finds you in good spirits. Apologies for the rushed nature of this. I am practically beside myself with glee and sorrow.

Where to begin?

After the last letter the search party returned with good and ill tidings. The surveyors had been found holed up in a cave. They were attacked by a pack of ravenous red wolves. Three men were lost, bringing the crew down from nine to six. Much of the equipment was lost as well but compared to the three souls that have left us it is a small price. Though the company men higher up do not see it that way. It is a shame when life is worth less than coal. A damn shame.

But the surveyors managed to retain their maps and we will begin to make our plans after the bodies are laid to rest.

On that note, in tragic news, Jeffrey has succumbed to his illness. He passed last night in his sleep. The sudden screams from his quiet room awakening all of us and caused a mad scramble to his side. In his sickness he managed to open his window yet again. When we got to him his body, though just expired was as cold as ice and tinged in blue. His lips darkened deep red as if chapped severely. A rictus scream of pain frozen on his face. It shall haunt me seeing him that way. All memories of him standing strong and fierce replaced by that look of terror. The doctors came to see his corpse and quickly whisked him away.

I got into a great tussle with them over his remains. They insist he be burnt to ash instead of sent home for a proper burial in consecrated ground. They insist all of the bodies be burnt as a matter of fact. No answers given as to why, just solemn marks of the cross from their overly superstitious hands. This whole land feels like it has not progressed since before the War of the States. Simple minded god fearing folk set in their ways.

I wonder what they would say about you here my love. Would their old ways send them into a fit of apoplexia at a negro woman and white man finding love together? Possibly. I'm not sure they even know of the emancipation of the slaves here. There are only two last names on the mountainside and neither seems willing to crossbreed with the other. Needless to say, I'm glad you are safely at home and far from these savage fools and their untempered belief.

I must go. They say the bodies must be burned within a strict time frame according to scripture. No scripture I have ever read. It makes me long for the civility of the city. The more open minded people, future thinking and prone to science over magic. I've given my notice to the bosses that this will be my last job and then home to retirement and start our family. They raised a great ballyhoo over this. Claimed I'm leaving them in a lurch with the sudden loss of Jeffrey. I don't care. We can plant crops and I can pen my manuscript of the outlying regions of our great nation. My life is with you, not them.

It should be a week, possibly two before I can return to our home. First to lay these brave men to rest. Then to plan out the mines.

I miss you greatly my love. And I will be there soon. Until that moment I shall write to you and keep you detailed on this cursed trip.

Love eternally

H. October the 3rd, 1878

My Dearest

The dreams are back again. Everyone is on edge. The tapping at my window occurred again two nights in a row now. Even in my dreams I am too frightened to peer out the curtain and see that blue skinned monster.

The townsfolk refuse to answer my questions about her. They will not acknowledge us when we leave the lodge. The first snows have fallen and now they seem to want us gone. No more than we wish to leave ourselves.

It's been four days since we burned our fallen comrades. Now another has fallen sick with the mysterious wasting away illness. The bosses refuse to answer our questions and work has ground to a halt. A contingency of fellow workers are talking about just leaving. The bosses swear if they do they will not be paid for the job. I've tried to be a voice of reason but there is none to be had in this hell.

Everyone is sullen and fearful. Jumping at every noise. I worry if the sickness doesn't get us, this eerie malaise will. Secretly I want to leave as well but we need this final lump payment to be able to settle down and start the farm. How I miss home. You. The clean salty air and tides lulling us into a sense of calm and security. The ocean is a balm for the weary mind and soul. Combined with your gentle touch it is heaven in a world of turmoil.

Two more weeks. That is where I draw the line. After that I will be forced to winter here and I fear I will succumb before it ends. The rooms grow stuffy and I fear what lies outside the windows at night. Two more weeks and I leave come hell or heavy snows. Until then I will keep the peace as well as I can. I will seek answers from the townsfolk in the meantime. Unravel this mystery ailment and ghostly blue girl.

I hear boots outside in the hallway. I must go and put out another fire it seems.

I love you my wife. Hopefully the next letter comes and I will be on my way to you.

Love eternally

H. October the 8th, 1878

Matilda,

My love how I miss you. This has turned from bad to worse.

The snows fall each night and soon the roads will be too treacherous to trust.

Neither boss nor worker can speak to one another without a threat of violence. Two more have fallen ill. One has passed on. I've taken to visiting the tavern in town and drinking until I pass out at a table there. This lodge has become oppressive with fear and hostility.

I've befriended a few locals. They tell tales of a group of blue skinned demons that haunt the woods at night. Evil things with fangs and blackened lips that lure men to their doom. It is said they feed upon their souls and leave empty husks behind. They burn the bodies so they do not rise again. I don't know if this is just rural fantasy or true but it chills me to the bone and leaves me weak in the knees. I've decided to leave without the pay promised. Death is not worth chancing over living a fruitful life with you.

Even here in the bar I feel the call in my inebriated sleep. Hear the tapping outside the walls. I shall return to the lodge this evening and pack my belongings and leave at once. It will be my first time returning in days.

I hope to leave in the morning if the weather permits. I shall write to you before I leave to let you know I'm on my way to your loving embrace.

Love eternally

H. October the 13th, 1878

Matilda, my love,

I have been trapped in the lodge for two days. The night I came to pack a blizzard swept in and the snow is halfway covering the doors.

The sickness has claimed nearly everyone in the lodge. I have barricaded the door to my room and pushed the dresser in front of the window. I am huddled in bed with the embers of my fire slowly dying out. I have broken the furniture for fuel and am running desperately low. I need provisions or I shall perish as well.

At night the tapping on the glass has grown to a cacophony. In the halls outside I hear the scurry of small bare feet and insidious laughter. Low rumbling voices of men bed stricken with illness. And shuffling steps that stop right outside my room.

I don't know if this is a plague or some dark magic at work. But I fear if starvation doesn't get me the sick and dying will.

I don't know how to get this letter out to you. I'm only writing it to maintain my sanity and focus. If the snows fall deeper I should be able to launch myself out the window and land safely below. I'm growing desperate enough to try now as the sun begins to set and before the night horrors begin. But I won't. I can last one more night.

For you. My love. I will persevere this madness.

Love eternally

H. October the 15th, 1878

Matilda, my dearest,

I did it. As the sun rose and the voices stopped this morning I braced myself and jumped into the deep snow below my window. I twisted my knee and ankle but the cold has allowed me to keep moving.

I write to you from the tavern. The locals are worked up into a frenzy. They speak of burning the lodge down with all the souls trapped inside. I hate myself for saying this, but I agree wholeheartedly with the decision. They could burn the entire woods down and raze the mountainside as well. There is evil here. Deep, old evil. The roads are too covered and my body too battered to make the trek to the nearest train station. I shall have to stick it out here until I can make the journey. The locals say it will be three days at the least, a week if the storms don't abate. But I need to leave. To return home.

They are gathering kindling to start the blaze now and if I could, God help me, I would help them.

Please pray for their souls and mine my love. I beg of thee. This must be made right.

I love you with all my heart. I'll be there as soon as possible. I swear this.

Love eternally

H. October the 16th, 1878

Matilda,

What evil have they loosed upon the world?

The lodge lies in smoldering ruin. All those men screamed as they were burnt alive and echoed into town

I fear we have damned ourselves from salvation.

Now the entire town dreams of tapping on the glass. No place is safe. I'm trapped in a room above the tavern unable to walk. I hear them scurry upon the roof all through the night.

The barkeep says houses are on fire all through the small town as more fall sick.

I dream of blue skinned demons. A fever burns me up and it is the flames of hell taking me.

I should have said no. Left when I had the chance. I fear it is too late for me now. Too late for all of us. We've opened the gates and now they are free to run rampant throughout the valley. Possibly the world. What ever kept them bound to the lodge went up in smoke with all those innocent souls. We did this to ourselves.

Even now I hear the bare feet slapping across the timbers above me.

Know I love you Matilda. Now and forever. I feel the end coming for me. A group is leaving as the sunrises and I will try and join them in a wagon. If I cannot I will send this last letter with them.

If I'm not home in a couple weeks, you'll know what happened to me. I'm so sorry. I never intended to leave you this way.

Love eternally

H. October the 20th, 1878

CHANCES

The water in the tub was warm, just shy of hot. It offset the numbing cold of the blood rushing down my arms. I tried to shut the water off but apparently had gone too deep and severed a couple tendons. It didn't really matter. Wouldn't be my mess to clean up. Probably for the best. The eventual damage it caused would make finding my body that much easier.

As darkness clouded my vision I imagined the state of putrefaction and sludge I would have left behind. What was a little damage to the floor of the bathroom compared to that?

It has been so long since I got any real sleep. The couch is uncomfortable. The bed was too big. Three hours a night for as long as I could remember. Now a nice long nap awaits me. One without dreams. No more tantalizing glimpses into a life I will never have. We are born alone and we die alone. I just had the luck of living that way as well.

But not for much longer.

My last thought was of her as I faded out.

I didn't do this because of her. Not the rejection, goddess knows I have been rejected before. Too many times to count. Once for every scar on my body at least. I am a pro at it by now. Always the wrong time, I am the wrong guy, she was the wrong girl. There would inevitably be something between me and happiness.

Always my fault.

This was probably my first successful anything in a decade.

I didn't get to savor the taste of victory though. Instead I got to go to sleep. The red water began to spill out of the tub and it was beautiful. And then nothing. Sweet nothing. The pain in my arms, from wrist to elbow, a distant memory.

There was no light. No tunnel. No choir of angels to welcome me home. Just deep black nothingness.

I opened my eyes and confusion was the first thing in my head. A waiting room. Looking down I saw I was in a black suit with a bright blue shirt and my favorite bow tie. I saw the chain of my pocket watch snake into the jacket and pulled it out. The hands seemed to be moving backwards. My sleeve slid up and I saw the jagged open slash on my wrist. But I felt no pain.

A large red display on the wall flashed the number eleven. All around me sat indistinct shapes I knew probably were people. But that was about it. Couldn't make out faces, just a smoky kind of disinteresting quality that made focusing not worth the effort. I wondered if I was just a misty wraith to them. I don't care.

On my arm rest sat a scrap of paper that read thirteen. Guess it is almost my turn.

I could feel this vague sense of disconnect. Nothing seemed to matter. If I had to sit here for a year I would do it with no complaint. Because really, what is the difference? Sit here, dance like a monkey over there. In the end it was pointless. My wrists itched. That was the only real thought. They itched like crazy and I didn't have the urge to scratch them.

A bell rang and the display switched to twelve. A tall female form stood up and straightened her dress. For the briefest flash she came into focus. Dark skinned with a radiant smile. She looked at me and waved and I knew I knew her. But the details swam just out of reach. She walked down the aisles of chairs and entered a room in the distance. I couldn't say for sure which one.

Did I know her?

Meh.

Minutes or hours passed. I stared at the carpet in front of me. If you really looked the tufts of fibers seemed to be swaying back and forth. An optical illusion I am sure. It almost looked like they were little people rooted in place. Just clusters of souls swaying to and fro, woven into the floor. It should have horrified me. Maybe part of my mind screamed in terror. But it wasn't an important part so I ignored it and waited for the bell to ring out for me.

It finally did. A red thirteen flashed and I stood up clutching the paper. I looked around but none of the people became clear as I passed them down the aisle. I felt bad walking on the carpet, smashing the little guys and gals beneath my feet. I had the eerie thought maybe I would join them soon. Be attached to a section in a high traffic area, spending eternity being stepped on. If so not much about me would change. At least there was purpose in it.

What an odd thought.

At the end of the waiting room was a corridor with shut wooden doors. Opaque glass windows with no markings took up the top half of them. In some there were lights on and I could see shapes sitting but could hear no voices. Like an old building from the fifties from the decor. As I walked a door opened to my left and I knew it was for me.

The office was a plain, aesthetically neutral room. Gray wood desk, matching chair, no pictures, or cats hanging on a branch posters. Just the desk a chair and someone sitting and waiting for me. He looked like an accountant stereotype brought to life. Balding with an ineffectual comb over, yellowed button down shirt with what looked like coffee stains on it. Black suspenders and gold rimmed glasses that I imagine perpetually needed to be pushed back up his nose. A thin wiry mustache and a look of sleep deprivation in dark purple bags under his eyes.

"Please sit. I will be right with you," a monotone voice bade. So I sat and waited.

"Mr. Ennenbach, Michael David Ennenbach?"

"Yes."

"Do you know why you are here?"

"No."

"Do you prefer Michael or Mike?"

"Mike."

"Well then Mike, I am Seth."

"Nice to meet you Seth."

"I am to be your guide."

"Guide to what Seth?"

"The afterlife."

"Excuse me?"

"The afterlife. We used to have pamphlets in the waiting room but no one looked at them. It explained all of this. You are dead, Mike. It says here suicide in the bathtub."

I vaguely recalled that. My wrists itched even more.

"My job is to determine your status."

"I thought that my status was dead."

"No. Not that kind of status. Your eternal status."

"Oh."

"Give me a second to run the numbers."

I just sat and stared at the desk. The wood grain of the gray desk seemed off. Instead of rings it almost looked like variations of the painting 'The Scream.' If I really concentrated all I could see was screaming faces inlaid in the wood. I didn't like it.

"Please don't stare at the souls. It only serves to agitate them."

"Sorry."

That screaming part of my mind was growing louder. Still contained but getting the interest of other sections of my brain. Souls? Did I not imagine the people in the carpet? Were they trapped as well?

"Hmm. Interesting. It shows here you had a very mixed life."

"Yes."

"You also seemed pretty balanced. You went a little wild in your teenage years. Ramped it up in your early twenties. Wow. That is a lot of drugs and alcohol. A lot. Bet you don't remember those years very well."

"Never blacked out. Remember most of it."

"Well that is impressive. Still, you never did anything too horrible. Moved to Texas to clean yourself up. Looks like that didn't work out very well for a while. Oh."

"Oh?"

"Looks like your rough childhood left some scars."

"Literally."

"That is a deduction."

"Is that good?"

"Depends on how you let it shape you. Depression. Fear of intimacy. The death of your father brought a sharp uptick in self destructive behavior. Divorce. Buried yourself in meaningless sex. Hmph."

"Hmph?"

"Most of your sin was self detrimental. You never went out with intent to harm others. Was your objective to kill yourself the entire time?"

"I don't know. Yes. I guess so. I wanted to drown the pain."

"By all the things I am seeing, you did your best."

"It didn't work."

"It never does."

"So I learned."

"Why did you kill yourself?"

"I was so tired of being alone."

"Alone? In a world of billions?"

"Without someone to share it with. Billions of people but not one to love."

"Love. I see."

"What is the point of life if it contains no living?"

"I don't know."

"And neither did I."

"And so we are here."

"So we are."

"I wrote my feelings until I found myself repeating the same longing. The same hurt. Spinning new tales of misery that all came back to the same point. I was unloved and all I wanted was to be loved. It was circular. Unending. So I decided to end it."

"Do you think your words did anything? Made any impact?"

"No."

"I see."

I was done talking. It all came flooding back. The missed chances. The near collisions. The endless nights of writing idiocy. The inability to stop the flow. I had said enough to a world that didn't listen. It never came out right. My words rang as hollow as my talent had false. I was no good at expressing myself. I was wasting time in pursuit of things not meant for me.

So I did the only thing I could think of. I ended it.

"You were neither good nor evil, Mike. But you let the pain control you. Do you know how many poets end up in this room? All because they couldn't find the one thing they desperately needed to be whole?"

"I don't know. I was never all that good at what I did."

"Why do you believe that?"

"It never worked. Never reached anyone. Never."

"I see. Suicide is a heavy sin."

"I know. But I never really believed in any of that."

"Belief or lack thereof is not important. It is how you lived that determines everything."

"And how did I live?"

"A balanced life. Not good, but not bad either."

"And what does that mean?"

"It means right now there are paramedics trying to revive you. If you had been good I could offer paradise. Bad and it would be hell. But neutral?"

"You can send me back."

"Yes."

"Or?"

"Or you stay here. In purgatory."

"Doing what?"

"Running numbers like I do. Until you have accrued enough points to move on."

"How long have you been doing this?"

"Two hundred years. Give or take."

"And how much longer do you have to go?"

"I don't know."

"Fuck."

"So what is your choice? Stay or try again?"

"What will be waiting for me if I go back?"

"That is up to you. I imagine pain. And maybe a chance to make things better."

"What if I fail again?"

"Then we talk sooner than either of us would prefer."

"Send me back. Damn it. Let me try again."

He pushed his glasses back up and smiled at me. "Good choice."

"Thanks Seth."

"It is my job. But hey, do me a favor will you?"

"Sure. What?"

"Keep writing. And lay off the drink."

"I'll try."

"Now get out of here. There is a line out there."

I stood up and extended my hand which he shook. The door opened up behind me, the hallway was filled with bright white light. I took a deep breath and stepped into it. The sound of water running into the bath echoed in the distance.

Let's try this again.

T-Rex and the Baby Doll

this one came to me while driving down the highway the day I got burnt by high temperature plastic, I was done and in my pain I wished a t-rex would stomp out and wreck everything

Never once in my life did I believe that there was more than what I saw in front of me. Magic and fairy tales were nice diversions, and invisible men in the sky were good for a chuckle but I put as much faith in them as I did talking dogs. It isn't that I didn't want to believe, I most certainly did. It is just that there was no cause for frivolity like that. The world was a dark enough place as it was without all that mumbo jumbo mucking up the works.

I found a trade I was decent at. Found a woman that was good for me and I was good for as well. We tried to have kids but sometimes things just aren't in the cards. I worked my eight to five job during the week and spent my free time trying to unwind. I was normal. And not normal in the vanilla boring way, normal in the happy and content way.

That is usually when the cosmos decides to take a nice healthy dump on you. Or so I have found.

One day I left my job and did the thirty minutes commute home. Perfectly normal. Same route I take twice a day. Same traffic I fight at the same time. I was passed by the same red sports car that is always in a hurry. Occasionally there is extra traffic or maybe a wreck to mix things up. But not this day.

Everything was just as expected.

I got home and unlocked the door. The key stuck a little coming out like it always does. The hinge squeaked a little despite my best three in one oil or WD40 attempts, some things just do not take to fixing I had found. I slipped off my boots next to the table where I always set my keys. I picked up the stack of mail, mostly junk with the occasional bill for variety. Everything appeared to be how it should be.

I looked down for my cat who always greets me and expects her ear and chin scratches. But she was a no show. That should have triggered some kind of warning. But it didn't. Blissful ignorance I suppose. I called out for my wife who I assumed was manning the kitchen and preparing evening respite. It was Wednesday so it would be meatloaf. It was always meatloaf on Wednesday. You could set your watch to it. Then I realized I couldn't smell any cooking. Warning sign number two that this was not an atypical sort of evening.

Also ignored.

At this point the average person would probably be feeling the first hints of apprehension. But not me. I called out to her again but received no answer. Maybe she had run to the store. She always had something or other to get from the store. I shrugged it off and proceeded to sit in my chair and peruse my phone for any interesting nuggets my friends had posted online or new developments in the world. As was the case nine times out of ten there was nothing. Like I had in my stomach. I sent the wife a text to see how long she would be and decided to make a break from the usual and see if she wanted me to order some pizza. Meatloaf night be damned.

No answer came immediately so I was off to the shower. Nothing like a soak to ease the weariness of the day. That was where I was headed when I found my wife. Or at least most of her I should say. And bits and pieces of my cat. Shock must have hit me hard and I stood staring at the jumbled pile of remains in the middle of my bedroom floor. I wanted to cry out. Scream for help. But I just stared at the partially ground up remains of my loved one.

My loved ones, the cat was like family too.

This must be an elaborate ruse my non-screaming mind decided. I could see her wedding band on one finger poking out of the gore. At this point the ground came rushing up to my face at an alarming rate. Then nothing.

I would like to say the nothing ended and I woke from this terrible dream to my absolutely normal existence. Instead I blinked into the beige carpet and smelled the death around me. Coppery and putrid, the rational part of my mind said, it smells coppery and putrid.

Unfortunately my rational part was not in control, my screaming loudly and frantically side was. This went on for hours or days or minutes. Time really ceases to have meaning when in panic, pain and loss are the only emotions coursing through one's mind.

The neighbors must have heard me and called the police. I know I didn't. I was too busy screaming myself hoarse as I lay in a puddle of my own urine two feet from the mostly missing corpses of my wife and cat. That was how the police found me. Not the best way to be greeted on the best days, but I imagine it was about par for the course.

The officers were asking questions. I knew that. I could tell. But the words made no sense. I had gotten to a sitting position but that was the extent of my physical capabilities. I didn't have the ability to scream any longer so pitiful mewling noises were all that came out. I seemed to be rocking back and forth as the light glinted off of the diamond on her finger. Someone put a blanket over my shoulders. I heard someone else vomiting. A part of me hoped it was in a trash can and not on the carpet.

Priorities.

Eventually I was helped up and walked into another room. The words became clearer to my frazzled head and I eventually was able to offer nods as answers.

Did you do this? No. Did you see who did? No. Do you know anything or anyone who would do this? No. When did you discover the remains? No. Is there anyone we can call? No. It was endless and repetitive. I was waiting for someone to jump out and tell me it was a practical joke. For her to pop out of a closet, laughing and calling me an idiot for falling for it. Did you hurt yourself when you passed out?

No. No. No. No.

I don't remember much more. They were questioning me. A lot of people came in and took pictures and examined every nook and cranny. More pictures. More questions. Eventually I was in a squad car, not handcuffed or responsive. We went Downtown, that is what they call it I think. Downtown for questioning. It had been going so well so far they must have decided I needed a new room to say no in.

As we drove down the road I stared out the window. I wasn't processing the things we were going past. I was trying to figure out what was happening. She was gone. My constant and only. The love of my life. Her smile was the cap to the end of another crap day at work. The smell of her hair when she gave me my welcome home hug in the kitchen. Her smile brightening up the room. All buried in a pile on the bedroom floor and strewn with cat parts. The structure and stability of my average, regular life was gone. The scenery blurred as my eyes filled with tears.

That was when I saw the t-rex holding a babydoll looking back at me from an alleyway. Gore dripping from its maw as it stood staring me down. The arm not holding the doll lifted as if to wave at me as we rolled past.

This would mark the second time I pissed my pants this day.

I stayed quiet about what I had seen. Mostly because I knew it was impossible. And because I didn't want to come off as crazed to the people wanting to question me about the death of my wife.

I was released a few hours later and an officer took me to a hotel to stay at until my house was no longer at crime scene. My boss was more than understanding about my needing time off. One of the investigators brought me my phone and some clothes. I sat in the empty hotel room staring at nothing. It just all felt so surreal. I guess I was waiting to wake up and it all be a fever dream or nightmare. But it wasn't.

Days turned into weeks and there were no leads into what had happened. The best guess was a wild animal that left no trace had come in and mauled her and the cat. What I saw was the uneaten leftovers. It defied belief. I was innocent as the deaths had occurred before I got home from work. My alibi was airtight. My life was ruined but I was free. It didn't feel like a very fair verdict to me. You suffered a horrendous loss of which we can offer no good explanation to except for the fact that you did not do it.

No shit.

I eventually went back to work. I just wanted to slink back into normalcy. Everyone walked on eggshells around me and gave me those looks that one receives when their wives are eaten by unknown predators but they are innocent of wrongdoing. You know the look I mean. I sold the house. I couldn't bear to go back there again. All I could see was the past. I had nightmares where I would get home and go into the kitchen to hug her and I would find myself hugging the pile of blood and remains instead. I was pretty messed up but trying to go on like normal.

Months passed. I was nearly the old me again, minus loved ones and a house of my own. But nearly me again. I was driving down the highway like it had become the new habit. It was the same nearly everyday. Like clockwork we slowed down because there was usually a speed trap under the next overpass. As soon as it was clear the same blue sports car would race past, clearly in more of a hurry than the rest of us.

That was when a t-rex with a babydoll on its claw stepped out and crushed the little blue speedster. I slammed on the brakes and came to a stop a couple feet away from it. I assumed it was the same one I had seen on the way Downtown. Hard to imagine more than one clutching a baby doll roaming around. It bent down and ripped the body behind roughly where you would assume the steering wheel had been in two. It swallowed the morsel in one great gulp. Then it looked at me and raised its other arm in sort of a wave. I half heartedly waved back. It seemed like the right thing to do. It bent over and slurped up the other half and with a pensive look at me continued across the highway.

I drove like a bat out of hell home, seems I had wet my pants again.

Noises

-*I'm sorry that I couldn't tell you this to your face. Call me a coward or whatever else you will; I know that it is what I am. I'm gone, running far away from us and our problems. All of the smiles and tears, the fights and make up sex afterwards, I am running away from all of it. This must be sudden, a shock and a horrible blow to you but it is the only thing I have left to do. I had to. I can't go on with this façade. I can't get up and put on my happy face and try and tell myself that it is all going to get better and that I will fall back in love with you. It is all too hard. I loved you more than I have ever loved anyone before, I hope you believe this because it is the truth from the bottom of my heart. I just can't go on like this. One day you will think of me and the times we shared and smile. You will be married to a woman that deserves you, I will probably be alone and miserable for having run out on you. I am not strong enough for us, not half as strong as you and I know I never will be. Don't look for me; I won't be anywhere you would try, in any place you might check. I am so sorry for this, so sorry that you will never know how much but this is for the best for both of us. There will always be a place in my heart for you and the times we shared, a special place whether you want to believe me now or not. I know how this must look, my running off in the night and leaving you a Dear John letter but I couldn't think of any other way to do it without having to see the pain in your eyes. I am a coward and a selfish bitch. Even now, as I write this I find it hard to go through with it. But it is better to rip a bandage off with one quick tear instead of slowly and more painfully. This will seem cliché and ridiculous now, but I truly hope we can remain friends after the pain goes away and clearer heads prevail. But if you choose to not be friends I can only respect that and have no one to blame but myself.*

Love, Edith-

I found this letter on the nightstand when I woke up this morning. It was just over ten hours ago when I stirred from slumber and noticed that I couldn't feel her next to me. I stretched and reached over to her side of the bed and felt the cool smooth sheets that hadn't held her for a couple of hours. Trying to focus my eyes and wipe the crust from their corners I staggered out of the bedroom and into the bathroom. I checked the living room and the kitchen, but she wasn't in either. Then I noticed the little things that were missing from each room. Her little porcelain figures of boys and girls with oversized eyes and happy little messages of love and praise, the dumb little antiques she placed all over the kitchen, and the picture of her mother that sat on the end table were all gone. Panic filled my mind and visions of a robbery occurring as I slept swept through my mind.

I ran down the hall and opened the door to the garage and saw her car missing. I ran back through the house, past the dusty shelf with small impressions of the statuettes that sat for the last five years, and back into the bedroom. My heart was thumping in my chest and my hands trembled out of control as I opened the closet door afraid of what may lie inside of it. At first relief flooded through my body and my pulse slowed for a second as I realized her body wasn't propped up against the back wall. Then I noticed all of her clothes were gone. The shoes we spent three hours looking for at four different malls that matched the gorgeous black dress I bought her for our anniversary weren't hanging on the shoe tree I haphazardly screwed to the inner door. All of her blouses that I had teased her about and said looked like something her mom would wear instead of here belonging to a woman her age were gone. Even the ugly little shirt with the picture of Elvis playing in full Hawaiian glory was missing. But where did all of her things go I wondered. Why would a thief take her things and leave mine?

As I shut the closet door I noticed her pendant lying on the nightstand and the piece of paper beneath it. Confusion and worry filled my mind as I reached down to pick it up. I wish I hadn't. I wish I had not seen the letter under her favorite necklace. The necklace I bought for her on our three month anniversary. The same one I gave to her as we walked through the woods and smelled all of the flowers and laughed and touched and kissed and loved. That fucking letter and that fucking necklace sitting there and inviting me to pick them up, almost as if they were mocking me for thinking she had been kidnapped and all of her things stolen. That fucking letter and the words saying it wasn't my fault she stopped loving me and ran away. The hidden accusations it implied about me, about us. In an instant my world became nothing but cool sheets, dusty shelves and a letter that said everything I loved was gone.

I ignored her words and went out in search of her anyway. I stopped by her mother's house but she wasn't there. Her mother barely acknowledged me as I stood there, desperately signing and scribbling notes for her to read. She hadn't seen Edith, but she knew this was coming. They had talked, she stressed the word as if it could hurt me anymore than the pain I was already feeling, and Edith had been wanting to leave for a while but she didn't know how to. I ignored her veiled, if only barely, hostility and tried to plead with her to tell me where she had gone to but her mother wouldn't say. She said it was for the best for both of us this way. She said I should just go back home. Go back to our home that wasn't really ours anymore and move on with my life. She said I should look for a girl with more similar interests. I knew she meant I should find a nice deaf girl and twiddle my fucking fingers to someone who understood. She never approved of her daughter dating a cripple like me. She would even say it to her when I was in the same room. Maybe she thought I couldn't read lips, or maybe she was too much of a bitch to care and said it to hurt me and her in one swoop. I wrote her a final note before I stomped back to the car and drove off to look for Edith. I saw her read it and flip me off as I spit gravel and hit the street.

-Fuck you. I may be deaf but you are the fucking cripple. The ability to hear doesn't make you anymore of a real person than those stupid fucking dolls you collect. You are empty and fake just like them. Fuck you for judging me when you are too afraid to look yourself in the mirror and see who the truly crippled one really is. Edith always feared she would end up bitter and alone like you, but I think you always hoped that would be how it all ended. Then she would have to love you because she didn't have anyone else.-

Maybe I shouldn't have written those things. I should have been a bigger person, but I know Edith would have never left if it wasn't for her. And every second I spent with her anger and bitterness was another minute I could be out looking for Edith. I went to her job, and everyone smiled as I walked in. Her friend Cathy greeted me in clumsy sign she had been learning in class with Edith. Cathy only took the classes with her so that she wouldn't have to go alone. The classes were a surprise for me. Watching Cathy stumble over the greeting reminded me of the first time Edith signed for me. She took the classes for three weeks without ever mentioning them to me. Then one night she took me out to dinner and said she had a surprise for me. Slowly and carefully she formed the words with clumsy motions and tremendous effort *-I love you with all of my heart and soul. I want to be with you forever, walking hand in hand and growing old together-* I was shocked and began to sign back to her, but I went too fast and she couldn't even try and keep up with me.

But it was the effort she put into it that made it special. Seeing Cathy sign to me made it all come crashing back to me. Tears welled and made my vision blurry and she grabbed me by the arm and led me into her office.

I scribbled down what had happened and she sat back and read it all very slowly. When she finished she looked up at me and I could see the truth in her eyes. She had known Edith was planning to leave me. Everyone knew that she was going to run away from our life together. I guess hand in hand and growing old together meant only for five years or so. The look in her eyes made it all come out, the anger and sorrow and loss and pain poured out of my soul and ran down my cheeks as she wrote her response. She knew I could not read her lips through blurry eyes. I wish she had just spoken so I had an excuse to not see.

-She called me up two days ago and said she would be taking a leave of absence. She didn't know how long she would need, but she made it clear she couldn't say where she was going. She didn't want you to find out and come after her. I am so sorry that it turned out this way Philip, I really am. When she told me she had fallen out of love and didn't know how to tell you I tried to talk sense into her. She had always said how much she loved you, but when your father passed away things seemed to change. You grew sullen and distant she said. She wanted to talk to you but you wouldn't try and talk back. She cried as she told me it, I know she didn't want it to end up this way. Give her time and she will see how wrong she is, trust me.-

But deep down I knew she wouldn't see the error of her ways. The error was mine in thinking that she could love me with all of our differences. She couldn't talk to me because I can't speak. She couldn't love me because I can't hear. She didn't tell me because I couldn't listen. And I didn't see it because I was too blind to it all. Everyone else saw what was so hidden from me. And in Cathy's eyes I saw the look I had grown to despise growing up. I saw the 'poor deaf kid' looks that I always got from the neighbors and people who met me as I grew up. Edith never gave me that look and that made me fall in love with her. But I guess she had given me that look, just never to my face.

I thanked her and asked to tell Edith that I love her and want her to see me when she gets back if she wants to and left the office. I kept my head low so none of the others could see the poor deaf guy cry as he walked out of the office. Cathy walked me out to the street and gave me a hug which I limply stood and received. I didn't want her pity. I didn't need any of their pity. The only thing I wanted was Edith and she was gone. Hiding out and waiting until the smoke cleared and the stupid deaf guy stopped coming around looking for her.

I have read that when one sense is gone all of the others grow heightened. Never before had those words held so little comfort. I read it for the first time when I was a boy at the special school for disabled children my father worked two jobs to put me in. Those words gave me strength. I would pretend to have special powers of sight and touch that helped me solve crimes. I was going to grow up and be the first deaf superhero. With my super eyesight and sense of smell I would solve crimes and rescue innocent civilians from evil villains bent on world domination. There was no place they could hide that I couldn't see the smallest clue or catch the faintest whiff of their trail. When the bad guys used sonic weapons to cripple the other heroes, I would be the only one left to battle them due to my deafness. It would be a plus instead of the perceived negative everyone else made it out to be. When I saved the world I would teach everyone that you are only handicapped if you allow yourself to be.

But I had been wandering around blind for the last couple weeks as the woman I love grew more distant and cold. I didn't see the signs or feel the vibrations that said the world was coming down around me. The only sense that felt heightened was the sense of self pity that filled me up at that moment nearly four hours ago. It filled my stomach and crawled like acid up my throat until I felt like I was choking on it. The bitter taste of my failure and stupidity in my mouth and tears soaking my collar were all I had as I drove to the empty house that was once a home. When I looked at myself in the rear view mirror I saw my own face making that poor deaf guy face back at me. It was right then I knew there was only one thing left for me to do.

When I returned to our, my, house I was shocked at how easily she was able to remove herself from it. All traces of her were gone and everything else looked just like normal. But it wasn't normal at all. My eyes went to the spots where her things should have been automatically, everything else ceased to exist. Those voids in the rooms called out to me and begged me to stare at them. It wasn't as if she had taken the couch or the computer and desk, nothing major was missing at all. But the picture of her as a little girl sitting on her uncle's horse with her hair in pig tails wasn't on the desk any longer. The coffee table was in the same spot as always but the book she had been reading for the last two months wasn't on top of it. I walked around like a zombie and noticed everything that wasn't there. It had only been five hours since I read her letter but it felt as if an eternity had passed.

She was gone and I was to blame. I should have seen the signs. She had been distant and standoffish for the last few days but I didn't pay it much attention. She always went through little phases like that. Besides, I had been in the middle of writing my latest short story and I always get so focused into that that the world around me fades into the background. She used to wait up for me if I was writing late, but lately she had just started to go to bed without even coming in and giving me a kiss goodnight. I have always been too self absorbed, ever since I was a child I have been this way. If I had some kind of concrete goal in front of me that was the only thing I saw. But I should have seen the distance between us growing. I should have been more attentive to her and the feelings she was losing.

Maybe I could have stopped the downward slide of our love, convinced her to give me another chance. Or maybe nothing I would have done would have made a god damned difference to her in any way.

Maybe she just got sick of the deaf boyfriend that didn't pay attention to her enough. The deaf man who couldn't have a conversation with her couldn't hold her love.

Maybe she needed to hear the words I love you said to her.

Maybe reading it on a pad or having it signed didn't give her the chills down her spine she was looking for. She probably wanted someone who was complete and could sing to her like Cyrano, or recite poetry outside of her window like Romeo.

Maybe it was I who was too stupid to see that it was destined to fail. I had never had much luck with the women of my life, why should the lovely Edith be any different? My women troubles started when I was a baby. Pretty much right from birth the entire 'fairer' sex decided I wasn't worth the effort.

My father met my mother when they were both fresh out of high school. They had dreams and goals that they wanted to pursue. Mother came from a rich family back East and had wanted for nothing her entire life. Dad came from a working class family on the West coast and made up for the lack of money with drive and brains. They met in a chance encounter at a small pizza place in downtown Chicago. Dad always said that the minute she walked in every eye in the building was glued to her. She strolled through the front door like an angel, he would say. Beautiful and confident, with long blonde hair like spun gold and the most dazzling eyes he had ever seen. As he sat there and watched her, three different guys walked over to her and tried to ask her out but she shot each one down without batting one of her blue eyes. One of them was his best friend, Charlie, and Dad said he never laughed as hard as he did when Charlie came back to the table and tried to convince him that she was a lesbian. Charlie got so mad his face turned bright red as he stormed out of the restaurant and Dad was left with the entire pizza to himself.

He was about to box it up and take it home as a peace offering to Charlie when he heard a voice behind him say, "Would be a shame to let that thing go to waste wouldn't it?"

He turned around and his jaw dropped to the floor when he saw that it was that same beautiful woman who had just shot Charlie down talking to him. He would smile and stare off into the distance as he told me how he couldn't even talk with her that close to him, all he could do was nod and offer her Charlie's seat which she gladly took. They ate the entire pizza and ended up talking all the way until the restaurant was about to close down for the night. After that they were nearly inseparable, spending every moment they could together over a three year period that ended with them getting married in a church three blocks down the road from the same pizza place that they met at. Charlie ended up being Dad's best man at the wedding and made sure everyone knew that if it wasn't for his getting rejected by my mother, they would have never met.

A little over a year after they were married was when they found out that Mother was pregnant, the both of them overjoyed at the thought of having a child. Dad had just landed a job working for an investment firm and he and Mother made the down payment on their new suburban home. It seemed everything was going according to plan and the two of them were happier than they ever imagined. Then I came along and fucked the whole thing up for them. At first it didn't appear anything was wrong with me, that I was a normal healthy baby boy. It wasn't until they got me in for testing that it became obvious something was wrong with me. Mother was in shock when she learned that I was born deaf. Her parents gave her and Dad all the money they needed for operations to try and give at least partial hearing to me, but nothing worked. It was around my one year birthday when my mother decided that it was too hard. She couldn't handle raising a deaf son. She and Dad got into huge fights over me, she wanted to just give me up for adoption and try again but he wouldn't hear it. Soon after she filed for divorce and fled back to her parents leaving Dad with a crippled child to raise on his own.

Dad did everything he could for me to try and raise me like a normal child. But the cost of special schools and the stress of raising me alone started to take its toll on him. He did everything the right way though. He learned sign language so we could communicate and got me the best babysitters with training with deaf children to watch over me while he was at work. But this cost more money than he was making and he had to take on a second job at night to make both tuition and house payments along with the cost of someone at the house to watch over me. I never even found out the real story of what happened to my mother until after I graduated high school and started college. He always changed the subject when I would ask before then, but I could see the hurt in his eyes as he did.

Three years after I graduated from college I got my first anthology published to rave reviews. Dad was my biggest fan and made a point of being the first one in line at my book signing. I sat there for three hours signing books to all sorts of different people and finally I got to the end of the line. The only person left was an older woman with long gray hair who stood patiently waiting until the person ahead of her finished and walked away. She came up to the table with the book in her hands and awkwardly signed

–Hello Philip, you probably don't have a clue who I am but I am your biggest fan–.

I was flattered that someone in line took the time to actually sign to me, most of the people in line just smiled at me and shook my hand while telling my assistant who to make it out to.

I gave her a big smile and signed back- *Well thank you very much, who would you like this made out to?-*

There was a long pause as she tried to remember what the proper signs were. I could see the nervous way she looked at me as she began and I patiently gave her all the time she needed. *–Just sign it, To Mom, love Philip.-*

I was floored. After all these years she just decided to waltz back in and get a book signed. She never tried to contact me at all over the years and then had the audacity to walk in and ask for an autograph. I looked over at my assistant and carefully told her to tell this woman that I believed she was mistaken, my mother had died a long time ago. I watched her face as she heard the words. I saw her lips moving unintelligibly and her fingers giving little jerks as she tried to respond both verbally and through sign to no avail. I told me assistant that I was done signing books for the day and carefully packed my things and got up from the table. Mother tried one last time to talk to me, maybe she wanted to explain why she ran out on her husband and her little cripple child. I didn't care: I had nothing to say to her. She made one last attempt to grab my arm when security came over to restrain her and pull her away. That was the first and last time I ever saw her, the stranger who claimed to be my mother.

Virginia was the next one to walk in and out of my life in a storm of emotions. We met during my third grade year at school. I can still see her walking into the classroom on the first day of the new classes. She was taller than the other girls in the class and twice as pretty. This was her first year at an all deaf school and it showed in her green eyes as she looked out at all the faces with fear and trepidation. I didn't understand that look in her eyes; none of us ever looked like that here. This was our safe haven from the looks the regular people gave us. We were all united in silence, comrades who didn't even think to judge each other as cripples or disadvantaged. Disadvantaged was the new term for kids like us, sort of like handicapable, it was just a new spin on an old negative. But none of us thought about it that way. As far as I could tell it was the same as a normal school just quiet. And there she stood before us with understanding beginning to dawn in those lovely green eyes. Of course they were just gross old girl eyes to me then.

It didn't take her long to win over the entire class, which ruffled my feathers more than a little bit. Before she walked in,

I was king of the roost and I didn't have it in me to want to share that title. The best way to describe it would be dislike at first sight. As the year went on we began to compete against each other for the best marks on tests and projects, the best scores and times at gym class, and all around best in show at everything else. If I had been a few years older and had read a few more books I would have seen that we were destined for each other from the start. I couldn't stop thinking about her. At first it was with disdain and anger at the nerve of her trying to take over my class. Then slowly I was just thinking about her. By the time sixth year started, our third together, we had decided to pool our talents together and agreed to rule the class equally. I blame it all on puberty and the changing hormones raging within us. Soon we became inseparable best friends. At the start of eighth grade we were officially boyfriend and girlfriend.

Time seemed to fly by the minute we began dating. It was all innocent and fun then. We would go rent movies and laugh at the closed captions for hours on end. Guns go BANG! Engines would REV down the streets while explosions went BOOM. It was funny to us how the film industry tried to make it all accessible and it was just a big joke. Every time the captions would describe the noises we couldn't hear we would look at each other and break out into fits of silent laughter. I wish I could have heard her laugh just once. The way her face would crinkle up in the corners and her hand would delicately cove her mouth was one of the most beautiful things I had ever seen. I can only imagine that the sound that accompanied it was pure happiness. When we were at school together I made up some eight by ten signs that had the words boom and rev and bang on them and when I passed a classroom she was in I would hold one of them up for her to see. It was our own little in joke.

Her parents and my father hit it off excellently when they finally met each other during our second year at high school. Her parents weren't deaf and they had a lot to talk about with my father. I imagine they talked about the hardships of having disadvantaged children or some other shit like that while we snuck upstairs and tried to cautiously make out for a few minutes before one of them decided to look for us. Being deaf makes it difficult to sneak around, you can't hear them coming so it isn't really you being sneaky at all. We never had sex though, just hot and heavy petting over the clothes. There was no doubt in either of our minds that we would one day marry and figured why not wait until then. Why not wait until then? I really truly believed that we would always be together; it seemed like some kind of destiny that we were meant for each other. Then came graduation and all the shit hit the proverbial fan.

Three weeks after graduation Virginia showed up early in the morning to my house and woke me up. I saw she was excited and agitated and tried to calm her down. She was signing at a million miles an hour and my unfocused sleep filled eyes couldn't keep up with the blur of motion. I will never forget the words she signed.

-My dad just got off the phone with the doctor. He says that there is a new experimental surgery that may be able to let me hear! I am the prime candidate! Isn't that great! They may be able to fix my ears!-

I was shocked. It was great news, it really was. But I was scared too. What if it worked and she didn't have any use for a deaf guy any longer? She could find herself a nice normal guy who could talk to her and whisper in her ear sweet nothings and take her away from me. She laughed when I signed these fears to her. She would never leave me she promised. If it worked for her it might work for me and then we could travel the world and listen to music and actually hear a motor rev. It seemed like a great idea in practice, but it didn't lessen my fears in the slightest. I felt the foundation of my happy little world beginning to crumble beneath me at that very moment. The butterflies in my stomach began dive bombing and I couldn't help but feel that this was not going to turn out very well at all. But I left these thoughts locked up inside, there was no point in ruining her excitement over stupid fears and inadequacies, right?

I looked up at the digital clock on the bureau and was shocked to see how much time had slipped away in my quiet reverie. It had now been almost seven hours since I had awoken alone to an empty home. The fresh wounds from Edith were dredging up pain from long ago. I had walked into the house from Edith's work almost two hours ago and sat down in my recliner and fallen backwards through time without even realizing it. I should have started writing all of this down. Making a definitive map of self loathing and sorrow for others to read and figure out the proper paths to avoid if they found themselves walking down the same trails. It would be a lie to say I hadn't thought about Virginia in a long time, I did nearly every day. Even at the best times with Edith I would awaken in the middle of the night from a dream in which I was still with Virginia. Sometimes I would look over at Edith and think for a minute that it wasn't her sitting across from me. Even while having sex, I would sometimes slip back and think that it was really Virginia I was with. Maybe Edith had sensed this somehow. Maybe she knew deep down that I would always be in love with Virginia and that was what drove her away from me. All I knew for sure was that I was completely miserable and didn't want to deal with this pain any longer.

All of these flashes from the past, the hurtful reminders, the road markers of past failures, and the way I keep eating my anti-depressants like candy were making a volatile cocktail in my mind. Did I mention my penchant for pills? I have a great understanding of the demons inside of me, no control over them though which makes the pills act as a sort of lion tamer for my psyche. I never went to a doctor for any real period of time, just here and there to get some meds and then off onto a new cycle of hostility. The only one who ever really made me feel like there was hope disappeared for a while after his wife fell down a flight of stairs. I guess he and I were on the same page for a while there. I heard he started up his practice again, but by then I had enough stockpiled pills to last me for a while and my book writing had taken off so I could get pretty much anything I wanted from special sources. I am not a junkie by any stretch, but I know that my pain is what brings my readers back. I balance myself out with certain mixtures and let it all come out when the muses are with me. But the pills aren't working today. The demons rage in my mind and they must be silenced. That is why there is a locked box beneath my various pill bottles; in there I store the ultimate lion tamer. The tamer and I are going for a walk in the woods where I first met Edith.

I wonder about the supposed healing power of music sometimes. I have read different stories of how the sad songs make the hurt lighten. I have read the lyrics to some of these songs and found most of it to be Hallmark quality poetry. How could a simple song make someone feel better? Is it the fact that someone else has felt the same kind of hurt before? That you aren't alone in your misery? If so, then my theory of the ability to hear and plain stupidity gains credibility. No one understands another person's pain. They can't feel for you in your time of need. Your pain is precisely that: it is yours. The twisting knives in your gut don't travel over to them. They don't find themselves crying for no reason because they found that stupid little cup she bought at a garage sale and thought was perfect even with the cracked handle and faded words. No one could feel what put Sylvia Plath's head in the oven, the thing that drove her there. You may sympathize with another but you don't actually experience it. So how could stupid music be beneficial? There are times to run and times to fight, but the true genius knows when the fight is over. Pull in the troops, call the planes back to base because this fucking war is over.

As I pull into the state park I am overwhelmed with a flurry of memories of Edith and I. This is the place we met an eternity ago. I was walking the trails and just getting the city stink off of me when I walked into her. I literally walked right into her as I was turning a corner and trying to watch a squirrel scurry up a tree. I was in awe of its nimble prowess, the way it seemed to find every available edifice to climb without even putting on a slight show of effort. Then I felt the impact and a sudden freezing wash down the front of my sweatshirt. In shock I looked where I was walking and saw that the remains of the big bottle of sports drink that didn't land on my shirt was all over a lovely woman who looked anything but pleased to see me. Her eyes were open wide with rage, and from the way her lips were moving and the large amounts of spittle flying from them I am sure the words she was screaming were anything but pleasant. Luckily for both of us she was so enraged that I couldn't make out any of the things she was saying so no offense was taken. I quickly and instinctively signed to her how sorry I was, but she took my gesturing as an added insult and gestured back with the only sign non-deaf people seem to care to learn. I may have fallen in love with her right at that moment.

After a few minutes of her yelling and trying to maintain some small semblance of dignity she figured out I couldn't hear a word she had been saying. My notepad had suffered from the red spill of sport drink and I found myself unable to communicate back to her at all with anything but broad gestures. I felt like I was trying to sign to a retarded child, much the way she felt at trying to communicate with me I am sure. I helped her up and managed to convince her to walk with me the couple of hundred feet to the nearest concession stand so we could get some napkins and I could write a proper apology. We sat and scribbled notes back and forth and somehow I managed to convince her to go out to dinner with me as a way of apology. That was the beginning of our relationship and this was where it all happened. I can't think of a more fitting place to finish it all.

On nights like this with the sun just beginning to set earlier in the sky with oncoming winter months, the park tends to empty out quickly and I found I had most of the parking lot to myself. The sun was just setting and the play of colors from it across the sky and reflected off of the waters of the dirty river that cuts a path throughout the park were entrancing. I sat in the car and watched the swirls of pinks and purples play off of the blue and dank brown backdrops. I had dreamt of painting as a child but the works on canvas never quite meshed with the works in my head so I took to writing the scenarios instead of painting them. It was more fulfilling, I always told myself, to paint the backdrops with words instead of paint and give the reader the chance to imagine them themselves. I'm sure that is what every failed painter that picks up a pen and paper says to justify their own lack of talent. I wish I could paint a portrait of the pain and remorse that was flowing through my body. The regrets would taint the canvas and give view to the inner hatred working against the will to make it through this. It would more adequately explain my reason for coming here than a thousand diatribes of heartache could ever give justice to. The painting would be called the last stand of a tired man, and children all over the world would see it and know the power of love and sorrow have over simple men. It would be a warning to all against giving up the most intimate details of who you are to someone else only to have them rejected and discarded. But instead all I have is a gun my father bought for me when I hit it big with my second collection of short stories for protection from stalker fans. I am glad he isn't here to see the use I intend to give his gift of protection. I doubt he would approve at all.

My father was a great man. He gave of himself willingly to any and every person who needed his help. But when the cancer spread throughout his body there was nothing that could be done to help him. Even to the very end he was the strongest man I will have ever the honor of knowing, but I was luckiest of all the people he touched for I was his son. He kept the knowledge of his sickness from me until the very end. It wasn't important he said. There was nothing that could be done to help him, so why would he want me to get all worked up. He was just happy I

was writing, that I had a career and girlfriend and that he didn't
have to worry about me when he was gone. He would lie in bed
with a grimace of pain on his face and read my stories and smile.
He said they gave him strength, my stories helped to ease the
pain. I wouldn't cry in front of him. He didn't want to see it and
I wasn't about to let him down but it hurt so goddamned bad.
Knowing he was leaving me and not being able to do a thing
killed me as the cancer killed him. And when the call came that
horrible fucking day and said he had passed away in his sleep I
still couldn't cry. I couldn't break down and be a sissy and let
him down. I just gave praise to whatever powers blessed me with
a father as great as him. I celebrated the things he did and the life
he led. I did it all the way he would have wanted.

Edith knew how badly it hurt me to lose him. She knew it
ate me up inside and everyday the pain grew. But I wouldn't
talk about it. I wouldn't write about it. I refused to give it a life
of its own. I wasn't going to give in and let the dam burst and
emotion pour out. And that caused our separation. I see it now.
All the things I could have done to bring us closer, but instead I
pushed us apart. The little things I could have done to show how
much I appreciated her help and strength through the entire
ordeal that I didn't do. Maybe if I had shown her how much
she meant to me during that period instead of blockading my
feelings from the world I would have woken up to her sitting
up against the headboard reading a book or doing a crossword
puzzle. She would have smiled at me and clumsily signed that
she was ready to be taken out for breakfast. The last eight hours
would be a bad dream. The thoughts of losing her and dad,
Virginia and my mother, they all would be erased. But I am
not bright enough to have done any of these things correctly.
Instead, I sit here looking at the fading sun and feeling the heavy
gun in my pocket. Instead I exit the car with head hung low
and seek a nice scenic spot to blow the back of my head off and
end the façade. When I could have been strong like my father,
I choose to run and take the easy way out like my mother. I

wonder if she would be proud to know that her son took after her a little bit? When the going got too tough we both just ran to the only shelter we knew.

I chose the same path I had walked along the day I met Edith. It seemed fitting to begin and end the journey along this trail. As I walked along I saw a squirrel scurry across the path in front of me and for a fleeting second thought it may have been the same squirrel from all those years back. It was probably the son or daughter of that squirrel, his father long since moved on to wherever it is that squirrels go when they die. The years of instinct and born knowledge taking him or her along the very path their progenitor had taken as did his for centuries. What did he have to worry about? If there weren't enough nuts and berries to store for the coming winter, the people in the park probably took care of them. They didn't have to worry about getting evicted from their trees for not paying bills. No deadlines from editors, or solicitations from salesmen to wake them in the morning. All day it is eat some nuts, screw some she squirrels, then climb a tree and take a nap. I wonder if they watch us as we watch them and run back to the others and tell stories laughing at us after we pass. They have a good laugh at the funny shaped human and then all join in for a squirrel orgy, topped off with a breakfast of nuts and berries.

I kept walking past the squirrel as he took a sharp right off of the path and probably climbed some tree. I walked a few more feet and stopped at almost the exact spot where I had knocked Edith down. I closed my eyes for a minute and tried to remember the smell of the watermelon drink that drenched my shirt. I could see the look of hatred and anger that filled her face as she lie on the ground and screamed profanities at me, as well as that urge to break out in laughter, at the sight of it all barely held back by feelings of remorse that washed over me for a brief second. My hand went into my pocket and I felt the heavy gun my father bought to protect me, the same gun that would soon kill me. I slowly pulled it out and took a last look at the park around me. The scenic beauty of nature, the last thing I would ever see. I put the barrel of the gun in my mouth and began to gently apply pressure onto the trigger. It wouldn't take much to fire it; I had spent enough time at the firing range practicing to know just how little pressure it took to fire it. And as the hammer slowly began to pull away from the gun I saw a group of squirrels, five or six of them, rush past me with terror etched on their little faces. I stopped pulling the trigger and the hammer gently fell back to rest and quickly turned to see what had driven the squirrels down the trail. My first thought was a park ranger had come down the trail and would round the corner at any second and see me about to kill myself. This was supposed to be a private moment alone, my last few seconds alone with my thoughts. My eyes grew wide as I saw a tree quickly coming towards me. Confusion filled my mind as I tried to find an explanation for why a tree would be getting closer to me. The realization dawned on me as the tree fell on top of me. My last thought before dropping out of consciousness was as follows- If a tree falls in the woods and only a deaf man is around to hear it, it doesn't make a noise. Then there was nothing at all.

I have no clue how long I was unconscious beneath the tree. When I woke up I felt shooting comets of pain flying from my left leg and right arm. I felt nauseous from the pain, my head was spinning and I felt the root of another blackout taking hold. As I began to fade back out I swear I heard birds chirping and leaves rustling in the wind. Then there was nothing again. The rising sun to the east slowly fell into night as my eyes closed.

I woke up again to the sound, the sound? My god yes! I woke up to the sounds of park rangers asking if I was okay. I tried to give some sign of life but the slightest movement caused pain to shoot through me like molten lava. My head grew light again. But I heard them talk! I heard words and sounds for the first time in my entire life! My head was spinning from the sudden cacophony of the world and the horrendous agony of two broken limbs. One of them saw my eyes blinking and gave a call that I was still with them. I felt and heard the movement of the tree being pulled off of me and as I passed out again I had a smile on my face. They must have thought I was insane for smiling in this situation, but I could hear! I was no longer a cripple to be looked at with pity! I was complete.

Then I was unconscious.

I fell in and out for the next few days. I was not conscious long enough to ever try and communicate with the doctors and nurses, or the policemen who seemed to be in and out of my room. But each time I briefly awoke I heard sounds all around me. The gentle beeping of the heart monitor, the talking of people in the hallway and in other rooms, all of these noises filled me up and fluttered through my head.

It wasn't until the fifth day after they found me in the park underneath the tree that I was awake enough to talk with the doctor. The park ranger found my wallet in my pocket and the gun in the brush not far from where I had been standing. He stood above me with an interpreter who translated his words into sign for me. But I heard every single one of them! I tried to sign back that I could hear him but my right arm was crushed and in my sudden excitement I moved it and pain washed across me. I slowly signed back to the doctor that I could hear him. Looks of confusion passed across as they heard my words translated. I tried to speak but only a braying sound came out of my mouth. I had never spoken before, I couldn't even sound out the simplest of words. I was overcome with frustration at not being able to speak the words I had made my living with. The doctor placed a hand on my left shoulder in reassurance.

"You can hear me Philip?"

I nodded yes.

"Your records indicate that you were born with zero hearing in either ear. They show that you are one hundred percent deaf. This is some kind of miracle!" he said with a large grin growing across his face.

I felt a reciprocal grin growing on my own.

He explained to me that what happened out in the woods was undocumented in any cases in the entire history of medicine. He then explained that it could be a temporary state and to not get attached to the idea of living with the ability of hearing. He immediately scheduled testing to be done. I just sat with a stupid grin on my face as he said it all. I could hear every word he said. I signed to the translator that I understood the impossible had happened. I understood that it could be temporary. That I didn't give a shit, I could hear!

After the doctor left the police officers I vaguely recalled seeing in my moments of lucidity entered the room. They questioned me about the gun and my intent in the woods that night. Embarrassment filled me as I signed my response to them. They checked my files and saw that I was licensed to carry the firearm. One of them turned out to be a fan of my works and sheepishly asked for me to sign a copy of my third novel, which I couldn't do with my arm in a sling and broken in seven places but I promised him I would when I got use of it back. They filed the reports, and said there would be more questions when I was feeling better. The shock everyone seemed to feel about the miracle of my newfound hearing seemed to overshadow the stupidity of my going out there to kill myself. My lawyer came in and said he would do everything he could to get the matter taken care of with as little ramifications as possible. He seemed to believe that my agreement to enter counseling would more than erase the situation. I couldn't believe how well everything seemed to be coming together after how terrible it all had gone before. Soon I was left alone and I just laid there listening with curiosity to all of the strange sounds floating through the air. The hums and swishes of machines, opening and closing of doors, muffled conversations, all of these sounds served as the sweetest lullaby I ever had and gently lulled my to sleep.

Over the next few weeks I went through extensive testing and CAT scans but there was no evidence of anything happening

to my head to cause my hearing. I went through daily physical
fitness for rehabilitating my arm and leg, and speech therapy
classes to learn to speak correctly. It all flew by in a rush. I had
one of my friends go out and buy me a CD player and a wide
selection of different music. I heard the sounds of Mozart and
Beethoven, Al Green and Madonna, rap and jazz for the first
time. I finally got a voice to put with the image of Elvis. I felt
the rhythms and beats and understood the reason people dance.
I heard the BANG of a gun, the REV of an engine, and was
told my first knock-knock joke. Between therapies and talking
with friends I watched countless movies. But most importantly,
I heard it all. The good and the bad things all washed over me
and I was able to find out things about me I never knew. I liked
rap. My friends weren't too excited over this discovery but I was
thrilled by it. I liked the way country singers sang and allowed
the listener to hear the pain of their words. But I couldn't figure
out what was so great about all of the boy bands that had taken
over the radios. Even after weeks of hearing them play on radio
I couldn't differentiate them from each other.

My lawyer got all of the legalities cleared up about my
botched suicide attempt and the only magazine that reported
it was one of those weekly tabloids that no one really believes
anyway. My suicide attempt shared the cover with some half bat
boy child found in a cave in Venezuela. I did agree to go through
counseling as we had discussed, and I figured I would shock the
shit out of the doctor with the change from the deaf me who
suffered depression and the new me who longed to live.

The most important part of my rehabilitation came at the
beginning of my second month. The doctors agreed that my
progress and recovery were going excellently but they all felt I
should see a specialist who dealt with deaf people who gained
some sense of hearing. They scheduled a meeting between me
and the specialist for my first day out of the hospital. As I drove
out of the parking lot I reveled in the sounds of the city; the constant noise of passing cars and honking horns; the construction

crews and their assorted tools; the people yelling at each other in intersections; all got equal awe. As I pulled into the specialist's lot and walked up towards the door I was shocked at what I read. In big gold letters the doctor's name was spelled out in front of me, Dr. Virginia Stall. This was my Virginia. The girl I loved growing up. The one I thought of non-stop until the day of the accidental miracle in the park. She must have gone to college and decided to help out the people that underwent the same surgery as she had. And now fate had seen fit to grant me not only hearing, but a chance to see the love of my life. All of the pain and depression before had been a test and I must have passed with flying colors.

I was nervous going to see her for the first time in over ten years. I remembered everything about her. The way she smelled the way she smiled, and especially the way she melted into my arms when I held her close. I didn't know if she would be half as happy to see me as I was to see her. We had ended badly. We were young and I was stupid. No, I wasn't stupid as much as selfish and childish. I couldn't handle the fact that she could hear and I couldn't. I couldn't deal with being the cripple. She never acted that way but I assumed she would. I grew distant and standoffish. And when it came time to go to college, she was willing to go wherever I did but I told her it was time we went off on our own. I said we should make names for ourselves as individuals. And as she stood crying on my porch I told her she deserved to find someone who could hear her, someone that could be everything to her. Then I turned around and walked inside without a glance back. I regretted it the moment it happened but pride and self loathing didn't allow me to try and make amends. By the time I got the courage to try and talk with her again she was gone to the East Coast and I was left with my pride and hurt.

But now I had a chance to make amends. I could go in and apologize verbally for all the hurt I caused. I could try and let her see that I had changed. I turned around and got in my car and went home. Shame and fear got the better of me before I could even step into her office. I went home and started to write. And I wrote for hours and hours with no sign of a break in sight. I wrote of loss and gain. I wrote of childish stupidity and grown up feelings of shame. I wrote to her, my one true love in apology and regret and painted a portrait of a man begging for forgiveness and a second chance. I wrote the best work I had ever written. I wrote with honesty and true raw emotion. I told her what had happened since that day ten years ago. Of how I never got over her, never forgot her beauty, both inner and outer. I wrote and wrote, spilling my life out on paper as my drink had spilled across the park trail. I told her about my botched suicide and the miracle that accompanied it. Three days later I drove back to her office and slipped it into the mail slot in the middle of the night and went home to wait for a response.

The first week passed with no answer to my letter. I grew antsy and felt the pang of loss echo off of my soul as I realized that I had ruined something so perfect with a perfect finality. I started to write a new novel. This one was going to be a cautionary tale to the world. I began the tale of my life and all the wrong turns I had made. I wrote at a feverish pace, stopping only to watch movies and listen to music. I had fallen in love with rap, or hip hop as I came to find out was the proper distinction. I used the rawness of the music as a backdrop to my life story. I culled knowledge from Grandmaster Flash and the Furious Five, N.W.A., Boogie Down Productions all the way to newer acts like Atmosphere and Sage Francis. I felt the truth in their words. The picture they painted with words that were as vivid as great paintings and works of literature. The tales of the struggle and the hustle, they were plays told in five minutes. Poets and lyricists of the microphone that made lasting works and inspired my own writings so much that I sent a small piece to Rolling Stone for submission. My works were in heavy demand now; my story of gaining the ability to hear was the new big deal. My agent was flooded with requests for me to speak as an inspirational speaker when my therapy was complete. Everyone wanted to hear the tale of the deaf writer who could hear. All I wanted was to hear from her.

She waited an entire month to contact me. Her secretary called me and asked if I would come to a session and I agreed. My heart raced at the prospect of seeing her. I would finally get to talk to her, to hear her voice. To apologize and confess my love without having to write it out or sign it, but with real words spoken from my heart to heal the hurt I had caused so long ago.

When I stepped into the office it was as if time had frozen around me. All I could see was her standing there in her long white coat. Her long hair was pulled back and the strands were still fighting to go in front of her face like they always had when we were younger. I felt the same feeling for her at that moment that I felt fifteen years past. I felt awkward and stupid. My tongue weighed a thousand pounds in my mouth and my palms felt like a river was flowing across them. She just stood there for a long time, staring at me like I was staring at her and I saw tears well in the corners of her eyes. My vision grew blurry from the same tears blooming. Time stopped and she and I were the only ones in the room. My heart beat boomed once a second, filling my head. Then she smiled. I fell into that perfect smile, spiraling along in a torrent of love. The feelings of something missing from my life vanished in that smile. I was complete in her gaze.

I couldn't stop myself, the words in my head just burst out of my mouth and I said, "Virginia, I love you. I always have and always will. I was stupid and don't deserve your forgiveness but I will beg of it if I have to. I love you."

She looked stunned. I don't think she expected me to come right out with it. But I couldn't bear to play games; I needed to say the words that had been in my head for the last ten years.

Tears ran down her cheeks and I saw her hands trembling as they clutched the clipboard. I tried to silently will her to say the words back to me, to let me know she still felt the way I still feel.

Fear and anxiousness left an acrid taste in my mouth. I could taste acid in the back of my throat as I waited for her response. A headache began to pound through my temples as she stood there in silence.

"I love you too," came out as a whisper from her mouth and I felt the weight of the world leave my chest.

I stood there stunned; everything I had ever dreamt of had come true. But the acrid taste remained in my mouth and the headache grew stronger and stronger. I saw the world get blurry and felt it all start slipping away from me. I looked at her as I began to fall towards the ground...

...and I looked up. A haze of pain filled me. The taste in my mouth overwhelmed everything, coppery and acidic. I looked up and saw the trees, but how did I get back here? I saw the little squirrel on his branch looking scared, something must have spooked him and he sat frozen on the branch looking down at me. I couldn't hear anything. And my head hurt so badly and my body grew cold. I felt something heavy in my hand and looked at the gun as it slipped from my fingers. It was covered with blood and pieces of flesh. NO! IT COULDN'T HAVE BEEN A DREAM!! And then slowly it all faded to black and I felt no more. My last thoughts were of Virginia telling me she loved me too. And then there was nothing...

INFATUATION

Is this what love feels like? Whenever I see his face I feel my stomach lurch and warmness creep into my chest. Just the thought of his lips on mine gets my pulse racing. His rough manly hands and scruffy goatee are enough to drive me into a fit. I can't stop thinking about him. If I close my eyes I can smell his cologne, musky and sort of sweet. I can see the twinkle in his eyes as he tries to be clever. Or the way his jaw clenches when he feels slighted. I can't believe I might have fallen in love with the complete opposite of everything I have looked for. He is strong and manly. He is the type of man that wants to be the breadwinner of the family. He is the one who wears the pants in the family and calls the shots. My heart is pounding right now thinking about the way he extends his hand to help me out of the car. How he holds the door as we enter the restaurant and pulls out my seat for me. This isn't how it is supposed to happen. I shouldn't even be thinking about him while I am on the job. He is too distracting. And I am in love with him. At least I think I am. It has been so long since I have felt even remotely like this. Or felt anything except disdain for men in general.

Now this little bastard is lying on the floor in front of me and looking up at me with tears in his eyes. He is the kind of guy I imagined I would end up marrying. Look at the pathetic little fuck, all tied up with that tennis racket sticking out of his ass. As I look at him his sphincter clenches and the racket begins to slide out. He is doing it on purpose so I will punish him. They are all the same. These little rich boys with their six figure salaries come in and beg the mistress to hurt them. They spend their days ordering around whiny sycophants at work and come to me for a taste of their own punishment. They walk in and hang the Armani jacket on the hanger that rests on the door knob. They neatly fold their silk dress shirt and set the three hundred dollar tie on top of it. The nice slacks, tailor fit to show that they work out, are then placed next to the shirt on the chair. Then they crawl to me on their hands and knees and beg me to call them bad slaves and spank them.

Pathetic and tiring, but it pays the bills.

"Did I say you could let that come out of your ass slave? You will learn to obey your mistress, or I will hurt you in ways you have only dreamed of!" I forcefully remind the slave who is in charge here by tapping the top of the racket and pushing the handle back up his ass.

I feel dirty even thinking about **Him** here. I am supposed to be a tough as nails dominatrix when I am here. I am not a love sick schoolgirl. But he won't stop barging into my thoughts. Even now as I put the ball gag into the slave's mouth, I see him smiling at me from across the room. The crack of the cat o'nine tails against flesh reminds me of the first time he spoke to me outside of my apartment.

"Need some help with your groceries?" he asked me as I struggled to get them all out of the cab in one trip.

"I'm fine, thank you," I responded and then the bag tore open and my onions and tomatoes spilled onto the street.

"Here, let me help you. I promise I won't try and steal your stuff," he said with that Boy Scout grin of his. He just genuinely likes to help people, or so he told me. As he helped me get all of my stuff up to my apartment, I could tell he was going to ask me out. I was dreading to hear the words come out of his mouth. This guy is just so not my type I kept thinking.

"Would you like to go out and have a drink with me sometime? I know this quiet little bar a couple blocks from here that has an awesome jukebox," he said with confidence.

"Sure. That would be nice," I answered before I knew what I was saying. What the hell was wrong with me? Of course I wouldn't like to go and have a drink with you. You are not my type.

"How about I meet you here tomorrow about this same time?" he asked.

"Sounds great. My name is Lucy."

What the fuck is going on here? Is my mouth ignoring the signals I am sending to it?

"I'm Roger. Well I guess I'll see you tomorrow," and with that he walked away.

I tried willing myself to scream at him that I wasn't interested. I tried to say that I would not like to go and have a couple of drinks with him, but my mouth stubbornly ignored my brain. I watched him walk off and I wanted to take off my shoe and throw it at him. But I didn't. I watched as he got into the elevator and disappeared behind the sliding metal doors.

"SHEEPSKIN! SHEEPSKIN!"

Oh shit what am I doing? That is the safety word we implemented into our sessions in case it gets a little rough for the slave. I looked down and saw that I was grinding my stiletto heel into his scrotum and I didn't even remember when I started to do it. I let up the pressure and watched the tears flow down his cheeks. I felt no pity for him though. In my profession pity is a four letter word for broke and hungry. See what that fucking man does to me? I can't even concentrate on my job without him barging in and screwing everything up.

"Did I get a little rough on the slave? Does he need to take a breather?" I asked with absolutely no warmth in my voice. These cocksuckers want it rough. They want to be treated like the common people they fuck with every single day of their privileged existence.

"I am sorry, Mistress Alana. Please forgive my weakness. Maybe you should use the beads on me to show me how weak I am," he asked me in his whiny little nasal voice. I slowly walk to the trunk in the center of the room and rummage through it until I find the biggest gauge of anal bead I have with me.

As I coat them with lubricant I wonder what Roger would think of me if he saw me doing this. He would probably never speak to me again if he knew what I did for a living. He is so old fashioned. He thinks that I am a secretary at some insurance company I pass everyday on my way to my workplace. I had to lie to him and say my boss was a royal pain in the butt who won't allow me to have visitors or personal calls at work to dissuade him from trying to contact me there. I almost break out in laughter as I think about my boss being a pain in the butt as I watch him force these two inch diameter metal beads into his own ass. If he only knew that the guy who runs the insurance company likes to dress up like a schoolgirl and have me beat him with a long board. He even supplied the board with holes drilled into the end to reduce the wind resistance, allowing for a harder hit. If Roger saw me in this leather catsuit and three inch heels he would probably laugh and ask if I was going to some kind of costume party.

"Now you will put all of those up your ass and bark like a dog for your Mistress," I snarl at the freak on the ground in front of me.

Thank god the anal beads are usually the end of my session with this one. He likes to bark like a dog and have me rub his nose into the carpet as I slowly pop each bead out. Usually by the third bead or so he cums and the rest of the beads fly out as his cock swells and spurts. Then he stands up and towels himself off. It is the same routine week after week. He stands up and swiftly puts his pants on, then the shirt and tie, and finally the jacket before handing me the three hundred dollars it cost to be degraded.

After his second visit, I gave him a price break since he isn't nearly as needy as some of the others that come to see me. As he buttons up his silk shirt I think about Roger again. He would never wear such an effeminate color like that.

He was wearing a snug fitting t-shirt when I opened the door for our first date. It said the name of some radio station on it and thankfully he didn't tuck it into his blue jeans. He sure wasn't trying to impress me, and I found that disconcerting. Most men tried to show off how debonair and slick they were on the first date. Not that I have many dates, but the few I have been on in recent memory were like that. They would show up in a freshly dry cleaned suit carrying a bundle of flowers that immediately went into the trash as soon as I got back. But not Roger. He showed up in his jeans and t-shirt with nothing but a grin on his face as I opened the door. Men have it so fucking easy when it comes to picking out outfits. I bet it took him less then five minutes to get it all out of the closet and get dressed. I, on the other hand, spent the last two hours trying to figure out what to wear for the date I didn't want to have.

I was frantic as I went through my closet and dresser. I didn't want to wear anything too slutty, but I didn't want to look like a prude either. The problem was most of my clothes were work related, not exactly what I would consider date friendly stuff. After the hell that was getting my outfit together, came doing my makeup. I was trying for the look of someone who was trying to look nice, but not trying too hard. Not full blown knock your socks off, but not exactly just got out of bed and not giving a shit. If a man had to go through this one time they would forget ever even asking a woman out. They would just sit at home in their underwear and masturbate to lingerie commercials. By the time I finally decided on an outfit that gave off the proper vibe and did my fucking make up I had approximately five seconds before he rang the buzzer to my security door. I looked at the clock and saw it was almost exactly the same time he had been here yesterday.

Doesn't anyone understand the concept of fashionably late anymore? I buzzed him up and tried my best to not wait for the knock on my apartment door like Pavlov's dog. When I heard his knock, strong and quick, I restrained myself from rushing to open it. Why in the hell was I so excited about this date in the first place?

"Who is it?" I asked in my best schoolgirl voice.

"Uh, it's Roger, you just buzzed me in," he answered with confusion in his voice.

"One second," I said as I watched him nervously play with one of his curly brown locks of hair. I made him sweat for a second before opening the door.

He gave me a big smile and said, "You look beautiful Lucy."

I had been called many things in the past few months, but beautiful wasn't one of them. You don't get called beautiful when you are beating a man and calling him a dog unless you tell him to call you it. It took me off guard and I couldn't think of a single thing to say back to him that wasn't mean and condescending. So I grinned like a fucking moron and blushed. I fucking blushed at him like a teenager getting her first compliment from the cute football player in the grade above her. I tried to say something back, but I couldn't get past the fact that he really looked good in those jeans. I didn't really pay close attention to his physical shape yesterday as I unwillingly agreed to this date and was pleasantly surprised at how good of shape he was in. Not that that kind of thing matters much to me. But it is definitely nice to see.

I decided to try the whole respond to his compliment thing again and said, "You look very nice yourself, Roger." I should have just kept standing there like a simpleton.

"You remembered my name, I wasn't sure you were going to. Look, I didn't pressure you into going out on a date with me did I? I'm not usually that forward and it has been bothering me ever since I left yesterday. If you don't want to go through with this, I understand," he said and his brown eyes melted away any thought of ducking out of the date. He really is a cute guy. He kind of has that whole farm boy look to him. Normal rugged features, honest eyes and great lips.

"No, I want to go out for a drink. After the day I had at work today..." I am such a fucking idiot. This was going to lead to unpleasant questions. I might as well have said I didn't want to go out with him instead of explaining what I did for a living. But I quickly thought up the whole insurance agency thing. It wasn't a complete lie after all. I did have the supervisor from there as my three o'clock appointment today. Maybe it was a slight bending of the truth more than an outright lie.

"Maybe you can get me a better deal on some renter's insurance. I think I am paying too much for the coverage I have now."

"Let's not talk about that now. Didn't you say we were going to go to a bar that you knew?" That was a real smooth transition. I managed to go from thinking up a lie about my job to sounding like a lush in one quick sentence. Fuck.

There he goes interrupting my thoughts again. I wonder what he would think if he knew how distracting he is to me? He would probably get that cute little-boyish smile on his face and that adorable twinkle in his eyes. Now I am running late for my three o'clock with my Nazi fetish client. No time to iron, so I guess he will just have to suffer through it with a Nazi officer in a wrinkled uniform. These guys who come to me know that I do not perform sexual acts and they are okay with that. They want to be demeaned, not gotten off, and for the amount they pay me to do it I would be an idiot to refuse. I can't believe I started doing this as a side gig to help pay rent while I pursued acting almost six years ago.

One night I was at the Exit on a Thursday and the dominatrix that was supposed to show up for bondage night called out sick. The owner saw me sitting there waiting for my date to arrive and noticed I was about the same size as the girl who called in sick and asked if I wanted to make a few extra bucks. I was a little hesitant at first, but he just kept raising the amount offered until I couldn't refuse any longer. I remember seeing my outfit for the first time. It was a one piece leather catsuit that zipped up the back and when I saw it, I tried to back out.

There was no way I was going to get into that and go out in front of all those guys. With a little convincing from the bartender, a sweet little punk named Sheena (it was forever before I found out she was named after the song by The Ramones), I got into it. I felt like a whole new woman standing there. Gone was shy Lucy. She was replaced by Mistress Alana, the hellcat.

When I walked out of the backroom and into the middle of the dance floor, the room went wild. The owner called out to any man brave enough to face the torments of the mistress of pain. I didn't know what I was supposed to do out there. I just sort of froze like a deer in headlights and looked at him. The owner leaned down and whispered, 'Just yell at them and call them pigs and smack them in the ass. These guys eat it up. If you get going good, signal over to me and I will bring out a whip for you to crack. Trust me, you are gonna do great kiddo.'

Apparently my nervousness was obvious to the crowd. A few of the drunk guys started to yell that I wasn't a very good mistress of pain. It really pissed me off to hear them mocking me. Something inside just kind of snapped and I started to yell back at them. I don't even remember what I said to them, something to the effect of if they doubted my abilities to suck it up and prove they had a set. The crowd went nuts when I said that. No one would come out to the middle of the floor with me so I went out and got one of the guys that was yelling. I grabbed him by his shirt collar and dragged him out of his seat and ordered him to his knees. To my shock he did, so I told him to lick my boots. As he bent down to do it I pushed him backwards and he fell onto his ass. Everyone started to laugh at him, and as he scrambled to get up I slapped him on the ass so loud it made my hand sting and the crowd step back. This guy had enough embarrassment and started to crawl back towards his seat and I gave him a swift kick in the ass to get him moving. The next thing I knew I was parading businessmen around like prize animals at a dog show. I never did signal for the whip though. That was a little much for me to handle so early in my career. I did such a good job that the owner asked if I would do it regularly on Thursdays for the same amount- one hundred and fifty bucks a night.

And thus Mistress Alana was born.

It didn't take long before men were asking if I would give private shows. I was shocked at how quickly they agreed when I said I didn't do sex. I couldn't believe they would pay a woman to beat them and abuse them with no extra perks involved. I talked with the owner of the club and he told me to do it, he even knew a place I could rent that didn't mind the things that happened in the room as long as no one got killed. He set it all up for me for a small cut, a managerial fee he called it. I didn't mind paying him a small chunk; he never asked how much I got paid. All he asked for was one hundred dollars a week. How could I disagree when I could make three times that with one client?

And here I am, six years later, putting on Nazi regalia and wondering if I am falling in love with a paramedic who grew up on a farm. It is funny the kind of twists life throws at you when you least expect it. But enough of this walk down memory lane, my client will be showing up any minute now and I can't find my Iron Cross. Everything has to be just right for the illusion to work properly. This guy has an obsession with the so called 'Master Race,' and likes to have me dress up as an SS Officer while he plays my Jewish slave. It seems sick and perverse but, for five hundred dollars, it is well worth the depravity. I just tell myself I am finally getting paid to be an actress and try not to think too much about the things I am doing. It actually works.

As I watch as the 'slave' cleans the room and puts everything in its place while I snarl at him in an awful German accent, I can't stop thinking about Roger. I wonder if my client can tell I am just sort of mailing it in today. He isn't showing any sign of disappointment in the performance, but I feel bad about it anyway. I should just stop doing this. Sure the money is great, but if there is no satisfaction from it there seems to be no point. I wonder if Roger wants kids. I can see myself pregnant and smiling while Roger babies me. I know he would too. That is the kind of guy he is. I can't believe I just had that thought. I must be going fucking crazy. We have only gone out ten times and I am considering bearing his children? I don't even know if he wants to have a long term relationship with me and I am daydreaming about children.

"You are worthless! The likes of you in the presence of one of the Master Race is a disgrace. You are just a pathetic little Jew! Fall to your knees and lick the soles of my boots!"

I think that Roger likes me as much as I like him. At least I hope he does. What do I do if he doesn't? I should call him tonight and see how he feels. But that would seem pushy. I do <u>not</u> want to come off as a bitch. I wonder if he is thinking about me right now. I bet he isn't. I bet he is sitting in his office thinking about football or that blonde that just walked past his window. Why are men such fucking pigs? I think I will call him tonight and tell him exactly what I think about him looking at another woman that way. What the fuck am I thinking? I am going nuts thinking about him. All I know for sure is this whole love thing, if that is what this is, sucks.

"Do you call that a proper lick? I will break your neck if you try and pull another goddamned act like that with me, Jew!"

"I am so sorry mistress. Let me lick them again. I promise I will do better this time," the little toady whines. I wonder what this guy's wife would think if she knew what kind of appointment he had every other week with me. He probably tells her it is work related.

"You had better not disappoint me again."

As he holds my boot I see the pale ring around his finger where the wedding band sits most of the time. Has he ever forgotten to put it back on before going home to his wife? She probably thinks he is having an affair on her. She is sitting at home waiting for him to come in so they can go to the synagogue together, but inside she wants to hit him. The fact that she doesn't is why I am in business. If she were to beat him for being a sick little fuck that secretly hates himself for being Jewish he would be the happiest man on the planet. Instead she keeps it bottled up and he comes here for a release. Is there anything about himself that Roger doesn't like? I can't think of a single thing I don't like about him. I think I will call him tonight. Unless that would seem too needy. Life would be so much easier if I were a self loathing moron like this guy.

Fuck it. He can call me if he wants to talk.

On our second date, Roger took me to a nice little Italian restaurant for dinner. It was real cozy and romantic. They had candles on every table that gave off a soft light that reflected off of the wine glasses we each held. I found myself stealing glances at him while he ate. He is very well mannered, and unlike most of the guys I know he chews with his mouth closed. He even pulled the chair out for me when we got to the table. He told me about the little town he grew up in. I watched the way his eyes sparkled as he told me about the trouble he got into as a kid. He is like a child trapped in a man's body, so innocent and full of life. He is completely unlike any person I have ever met. I was starting to worry that maybe he was married and wanted me as a toy on the side. But after we had a couple glasses of wine while waiting for the meal, I realized he was just genuinely great.

I told him about growing up in the big city with three older overprotective brothers watching my every move. He acted like he really was interested in my stories and it felt good. I usually never open up with someone I barely know like this, but he makes it so easy to feel comfortable. He asked about my parents and when I told him they had both died, I thought he was going to cry. His eyes got glassy and he told me how sorry he was to hear that. It made me sad that they wouldn't get to meet him. Then I realized I had just thought that and I started to blush. He got all upset when he saw my cheeks flush. He must have thought I was mad at him for being compassionate, or something. He apologized and I told him it wasn't him, it was the wine. I decided then to try and stop being such a tough acting bitch around him.

We both had pasta smothered in a rich red sauce with chunks of fresh vegetables in it. At one point during the meal he reached across the table to wipe a little sauce off of my lip. I felt a spark pass when he touched me. It was like a jolt of electricity that made every nerve in my body tingle. If he had asked to come up to my apartment that night I would have said yes. But I was disappointed when he took me back to my apartment and didn't even try. I almost invited him up, but thought against it. Don't want to seem too easy with a guy I had just had my second date with. He didn't even try and give me a good night kiss. As he pulled away I worried that he didn't like me, or that I wasn't attractive enough for him. I spent the next hour eating ice cream and obsessing over every detail of the evening. Had I done something wrong? Maybe I'm not his type. All I knew was I kind of wanted to be his type even if he wasn't necessarily mine. I also knew I wasn't fooling myself very well.

When he called me the next night and thanked me for a wonderful evening, my heart started racing like a champion race horse. We talked for a little while and he told me he did want to give me a good night kiss, but he was worried his breath smelled like garlic and decided not to. I played the shy little girl and told him I didn't really mind garlic. I could tell by his tone that I had made him blush. I wanted to say how cute it was, but I didn't want him to not try next time. We playfully joked back and forth like teenagers for a little while and he asked if I would like to go see a movie in a couple of days. I acted like I was thinking about it for a second, not too eager, and then said yes. I heard him exhale as if he was holding his breath until I answered. Then we spent the next ten minutes trying not to be the one who ended the call. I felt pathetic and tingly the rest of the night.

I don't have a lot of girlfriends. Most of them are annoying little bitches that try and stab you in the back when they think you aren't looking. But Ginger and I have known each other since high school and she is probably my best friend in the whole world. When I got back from my fourth date with Roger, I rushed into my apartment and called her to tell her about it. My heart was beating and that tingly feeling was back again. We had spent almost a half an hour in his car talking before I came in. Alright, maybe most of that time was spent kissing.

Oh my god, he is such a good kisser! His lips are so soft and full and he knows exactly how to use them. He is so good that I had to ask him if he spends most of his day kissing other girls for practice. He just blushed that cute little way he does and said he didn't think about kissing any other girl but me. I could have fainted; I was so happy.

"So how was your date with Mr. Wonderful?" she asked me, her voice dripping honey that barely covered the mocking she was really applying in liberal doses.

"I don't know what you are talking about. But my date with Roger went perfectly. He took me to the ballet! He actually went and sat through three and a half hours of men in tights dancing. It was amazing! He was so polite and funny. He made me laugh so hard everyone in the auditorium turned and glared at me."

"Is he tied up in the bedroom waiting for you to get off of the phone?" She is also the only person who knows what I really do for a living. I think she is a little envious of Mistress Alana. She always wants me to tell her about my clients. She just sits and listens and cackles happily. Right after we graduated she met Jeff and they began a whirlwind romance that ended with her pregnant and him proposing. They are still happily married with three kids that are growing like weeds. She has been pestering me about settling down for years now and I always told her that it wasn't my style. She knew I was lying and never let me get away with it.

"As a matter of fact he is scrubbing my toilet while wearing a nice lace teddy I bought for him. He looks so cute, but if he snags another pair of my panty hose I will beat him half to death."

"Are you serious?"

"Of course not you twit. He dropped me off a little while ago."

"He just got onto his horse and galloped off into the sunset. When are you going to invite him upstairs and let him bounce your head off of the headboard?"

"Ginger! I cannot believe the foul things that come out of your mouth sometimes. Do you kiss your children with that thing?"

"Excuse me; I forgot I was talking to Miss Prim and Proper. Did you kiss him yet?"

"Oh my god, yes! He is the best kisser I have ever met. I wanted to melt into a pile of goo in his front seat."

"But he didn't try and see how much of you had gotten all gooey?"

"Ginger! I am not that kind of girl! He didn't even try and touch me. All we did was kiss for about a half an hour."

"Maybe they grow them differently on the farm than up here in the city. Jeff was trying to touch things he shouldn't have even been thinking about on our second date."

"But you let him touch those things he shouldn't have been thinking about, remember?"

"Don't remind me about that. If I had known he was so damned fertile I would have taken a separate car on our dates. Don't change the subject though. Is he the one?"

"I don't know if he is or not. I feel so special when I am with him. I just don't know if he and I are compatible. We are so different from each other. He said he would like to meet my brothers."

"You told him they were in prison in Europe didn't you?"

"I should have. The last thing I need is for him to meet the three assholes. They will end up telling him every stupid thing I have ever done."

"Did you tell him about your job?"

"I told him I have a job. He thinks I work for an insurance agency."

"Shit, you need to have insurance doing the things you do to those poor men."

"Funny, bitch. You think you are so funny."

"I'm just playing with you sweet heart. But don't you think you should tell him before he finds out on his own? It might not be so sweet if he finds out about Mistress Alana from one of his friends after they see the two of you out somewhere."

"I know. I need to tell him about my job. I just worry that he won't want to see me again if he knows what I do to make rent."

"But if you and he aren't even, what did you say? Compatible. If the two of you aren't compatible what difference does it make? You just need to be honest with him."

We talked for a couple of hours. She kept giving me shit, and at one point started singing a song about me and Roger in a tree. She is the only one who can get away with shit like that. Anyone else would get a punch in the jaw. Well, maybe Roger could get away with it. I don't know why I can't get him out of my mind. She told me about the kids and Jeff. They were happy and doing well. Jeff said he wanted to meet the man who might just finally make me an honest woman. I hate those two sometimes. But in the way everyone hates their loved ones. I wonder if Roger has told any of his friends about me yet.

"Mistress Alana, I have finished cleaning the bathroom with my toothbrush."

"Now walk back into that bathroom and use it on your teeth, you pig! Do not make me have to use the bamboo cane on your back. Remember the welts you got the last time?"

"Yes mistress, I remember deserving them for being a dirty Jew. I will do as you say, I am a good slave."

This is usually the wind down of his session. He spends most of his time doing menial tasks, and then when his time is almost up he likes to clean the rim of the toilet with his toothbrush and use it on his teeth afterwards. I wonder what his parents didn't do for him as child. Was his mother the dutiful housewife that cleaned everything before his father came home? Maybe he was brought up that men shouldn't be made to clean and now he feels dirty cleaning. I don't get paid to analyze the clients, just to make them feel inferior and small. This guy should be one of my favorite clients. He is low maintenance and loves to clean; if only it weren't for the whole Nazi/Jew fantasy he harbors. I would probably owe him money for cleaning up the lair so well. He doesn't even ask me to constantly yell at and belittle him.

Some guys come to me for punishment because they get off on it, others like him come here for penance for things they do in the real world. I wonder what it is he is trying to clean in his life that he gets some satisfaction by cleaning my lair. Who cares? Now I get to go into the bathroom and watch him brush his teeth while I slap him on the ass with a piece of salted leather until tears run down his cheeks. That is all he asks at the end of every session, just to be slapped until he cries. Then he lays an envelope of money on the couch and leaves without a word. He is almost tragic.

The key word is almost, I don't really feel a lot of pity for him. At least not in the normal sense that most people feel pity for someone. I pity him because I see the real him that he keeps hidden. Because I know there really isn't more to him than feelings of hatred and sorrow. But I am not getting paid to think about these things. So I began to administer his fifty lashes and try and get my head together. And not think about you know who. I am not having much success with either of those things.

Since my head is clearly not in my work today, I am considering canceling the rest of my appointments and just going home to sit by the phone in case someone should happen to call. I also cannot stand my last appointment of the day. He is one of those guys who comes from old money and holds a spot on almost every single company's board of directors from here to Hong Kong. He likes to be roughed up. On some days it is okay to smack a grown man in the face with a dildo, but it is really one of those mood things. The only good thing that has come out of my time with this masochist is I have taken three swings off of my golf game. Of course since I don't play golf at all this is just an educated guess, but I figure if I can insert a golf tee into a man's asshole and hit a golf ball off of it, I must be showing improvement.

When he first came and asked me to put the special tee into his ass I was a little taken back. Then when he said to put a ball on it and swing I was more than a little wary. It is really hard to keep the head of the club straight. I have heard my brothers bitch about it, but I always thought it was just them making excuses for sucking. I must have left the biggest welts on his ass that day. I even got to the point of almost apologizing for missing, but I think he wanted me to miss on occasion.

I figured him out pretty well from that first session and when he showed up again I was wearing a real retro looking golf outfit and some two inch cleats. When I jammed the tee back into its special place, I put my foot on the center of his back and drove the cleats in. He loved it. Sometimes, it feels really good when you read a client just right and do things he didn't even know he wanted done to him. Other times the client is a prick and becomes very demanding. This guy is the latter type. It amazes me when a man comes to a dominatrix and thinks he is going to call the shots. Isn't that the whole point of going to a dominatrix? Don't they come for the whole loss of control and the feeling of domination? This guy comes in every two weeks and tries to tell me what he wants done. But he pays well, almost a grand a visit and it is hard to turn down that kind of cash. But I am not a whore! I am no cheap slut that does whatever she is told. Well, not completely at least. I am so fucking pissed off at Roger! He is making me question my integrity about my entire career. He is making me doubt the whole bit about this being an acting gig until a real one comes up.

I never wanted to make this my profession. It just fell into my lap. I didn't ask to be a good mistress who does these things. I am so fucking confused about everything. I cannot tell up from down anymore. Suddenly I want to be a nice girl. I want to be the kind of woman that takes care of her man at home. I am not fucking domesticated! I am not!

I refuse to fall into society's belief about a woman's place. I am strong and secure. I punish men who deserve to be punished. I am the dominant one. But when I think about him, I feel so safe and warm. All the things I strove to not become are running through my head every time he enters my thoughts. I think about making dinner for him. I think about taking care of the house and waiting for him to come home and ravage me. He hasn't even tried to get into my pants yet! Am I not attractive enough for him? Or does he see me as an equal and is taking his time with me so it is special? Why don't I know a fucking thing anymore? Why am I thinking about him again? I was just thinking about my clients and now he is there. This is getting to be fucking ridiculous.

I wonder if this is what being in love feels like. If it means spending every waking moment thinking about another person, and wondering if they are thinking about you too. Is that what love means? Is it that feeling of helplessness right before the roller coaster takes the plunge after the long, slow, uphill ride? It seems so unfair and so fantastic at the same moment. All the bad shit in the world just melts away when I look into his eyes. All of the dirty, disgusting things that occurred in the span of a day are wiped clean with just one smile. Tonight may be the night I tell him those three dreaded words. I worry he won't say them back. Or that he will look away in embarrassment. Maybe that is the true wonder of love. Maybe that not knowing is what makes it so special. The joy and newness of discovering that everything you didn't know you wanted was out there looking for you. I guess I will find out soon enough.

Maybe if he says he loves me that this really is love and not some stupid trick my mind is playing on me, I can stop making grown men stick things into their asses and live a normal life. Or maybe it will make it all that much more enjoyable. Love is a many splendored thing, kind of like a spiked choke collar and a rich guy with no feelings of self worth. No matter what happens, I will always have that and I guess it makes all the other shit okay.

PERSEPHONE

as told to me by Orpheus in November, this is the first thing I wrote that made me think of poetry as a viable outlet for me—M. Ennenbach

she was Kore, daughter of Oceanus and Demeter, some said the fairest in the land and the delight and joy of her mother's heart, goddess of seeds and crops

one other believed this to be true, and unbeknownst to Demeter, Kore's lovely hand was promised to him in marriage by Zeus, lord of the gods himself, as he was known to do

the land was lush, bountiful harvests year round, everyone was busy and happy and fed, paradise every single day, Kore frolicked and gave the seeds purchase in the soil

Mercury and Apollo both begged Demeter for Kore's hand but she turned them away, endlessly pursuing Kore until finally having to hide her away from the prying Olympian eyes

then one day, in the blink of an eye Kore had gone away, stolen away without a trace, taken to a kingdom far, far away and Demeter was more than dismayed the winds began to cool and become bitter, the foliage changed color as the green faded away, crops began to wither and die as if the dirt felt the anguish as well

the people had never experienced this, warm winds and rain were to be expected, the eternal loving touch of Demeter always graced the land, nurturing and providing

soon the leaves fell as the

temperatures began to plummet, the ground became frozen and too much to till as food became scarcer and scarcer

sickness and famine blanketed man as snow covered the ground, rot set in to the food stores and Thanatos became an all too familiar friend

Demeter was beyond rage and sorrow, her precious Kore was gone and nothing mattered to her any longer, inconsolable was her grief and pain

Zeus himself was begged to plead sense to Demeter, to have her bring back the warmth, lay her hands lovingly upon the land and bring back the green

he tried and tried, plying her with every imaginable gift and promise, but there was only one thing that would bring life back to the ground, so Kore must be found

Helios, the sun, sees everything that happens, his unblinking eyes catching all that occurs in the world, and he came down to tell the tale to Demeter and force Zeus' mighty hand, to Zeus' chagrin

the Earth shook in violent heaves, like the sobs wracking Demeter's body as the story was told, until all that was left was icy rage at the game the gods had played, a blizzard sweeping their cave

Kore had been out dancing with nymphs and picking wild flowers in a sunny field overlooking the ocean, laughter and games, while the heady perfume of lilies filled the air around them

whence from the ground a black scar was torn and a chariot led by four skeletal horses burst through, a solitary man in black armor from head to toe standing tall and foreboding, the chill of the grave emanating

he called her by name and pulled her into his hellish ride, she flailed and fought but he was not to be overcome, the horses stamping their hooves and etching the ground in flames, their terrible cries erasing the laughter

back into the crevice they leapt, hoarse shrieks and the cold grasp of the Underworld flashed as the earth closed after them until all that was left was floating petals and the sound of wailing souls

Demeter screamed in Zeus' face, pounding on his chest in her impotent rage, her daughter taken by the Lord of the Underworld, separated by the veil of death in the arms of Pluto

locked in Hades, trapped in the land of the dead, far from the lands and the crops, away from her mother's loving grasp, alone in a land incapable of her touch of life and purity

the gods begged Zeus to bring Kore back, to end this insufferable cold that smothered the land, a return to warmth and prosperity, for as man suffered so do the gods themselves

finally cowed, Zeus sent Hermes to retrieve fair Kore from the Underworld, to bring her back and restore the balance to both humanity and the pantheon, to right this wrong

but what of fair Kore, alone in Hades, the Underworld, guarded by Cerberus the three headed mastiff of Pluto, god of the dead and ruler of these dark lands

her abduction and subsequent trip took a matter of minutes, the swirling memories of being grabbed and tossed into the black chariot, the largest jewels she had ever seen embedded all over it

the crackle of flames and scent of nightshade, the imposing figure in black so dark it seemed to eat the light rather than reflect it, helm with no face, just two jutting stag like horns

a single amethyst, the size of a young girl's fist the only imperfection in the perfect shadow form and bestilled yet its own perfection where the heart should be barely had she taken this in before she found herself locked in, for all accounts, a cell though filled with finery and accommodations, she suddenly found herself more alone than ever and aching for home

time passed, hours, days perhaps, without Helios it was impossible to gauge the flow of Kronos' purview, she huddled in the corner of the room wary and unsure, but steely resolve remained

eventually a letter was slid under the door, the envelope was addressed to *My Dearest*, knowing herself to be alone she guessed it was addressed to her, tentatively she opened it

My beloved, I apologize for what must seem like such a sudden turn of events and the haste in which you were brought here. I have waited for this day for a very long time you see

My betrothed, I have watched you from afar for so long, my curiosity turned to infatuation, infatuation into love, until I found myself consumed with the very notion of you and I together

My Kore, my obsession led me to Zeus, who persuaded me to follow up on my love for you, granting me the boon of your hand in marriage, now if you would, please join me for a welcome feast, allow me to explain myself

she was outraged at the audacity, yet intrigued at this faceless kidnapper, this love struck fool with the ear of Zeus himself, the lack of manners and oddly respectful tone, a puzzle to be worked

as children, all are taught to accept no drink or food from the Underworld, for if it were imbibed you would be trapped forever in this endless night, never again able to walk under the sun in the land of the living

ignoring the fineries and jewelry around her, Kore went as she was to the feast, cowered yet proud, escorted by beings wrapped from head to toe in silk and precious metals into a cavernous hall

the great room was empty except for a long obsidian table, candles lit with blue wisps that cast an ominous glow with no warmth, food of every imaginable type and the finest wines and a lone man at the end

she paused at the sight of him, sallow skin and pensive lavender eyes, the hint of a wan smile, she absorbed it all yet showed no emotion, her demeanor and back rigid, pride etched on her features

slight courteous words exchanged, pensive silence, the host enjoying the feast while the guest huddles, knees to chest and arms crossed, eyes staring daggers

she declined all offers of food and wine, of delicacies and lost vintages, all prepared with the finest touch, the greatest chefs to pass across the veil tasked with its creation

the lavender eyes showed hurt at first and as the mockery of a dinner went on it became a slow burning anger, all his attempts were stricken down, died stillborn in his mouth

finally he rose, walking towards her, mortified she tried to shrink in her chair, he reached down and grabbed her hand, cold as death, and pressed it to his lips

I understand your fear and confusion, but know I love you my Kore, this is your home and when you decide to take my hand you shall rule over this land as my Queen

he then reached over and placed a hand on the wall, the brick shifted and dirt poured down until one lone pomegranate sat in his manicured hand

forgive my lack of manners, it is not often I have a guest and my skills have deteriorated over time, return to your room, and if you grow hungry eat this, a gift from Gaia herself

with that said he kissed her hand again and recused himself through the giant platinum etched doorway at the far end of the dining hall, the chill following slowly

she stood and shouted before the great door closed, demanding the name of the man who took her against her will and locked her in a gilded cage *my dear, I am Pluto, ruler of Hades and god of death and rebirth, the silent of the three brothers, faceless Lord of the Dead, and soon to be your loving husband*

with that the door shut and she was taken back to her room, shaken by the knowledge of her captor and this prison, far removed from all she ever knew and alone

she sat, shivering and softly crying for her mother, how frightened and angry she must be, cursing Zeus for his tampering, and ate one solitary seed in her worry

eventually another letter was slid beneath her door, the flowing letters of her suitor, captor, and now adversary, tempting her again, begging to be read

Kore, our first meal did not go as planned, I hoped to sweep you off of your feet, enamor you with wit, instead I did nothing to assuage your fears, I failed you

come with me and tour our kingdom, this new world that you have been thrust into and suddenly become yours to rule, a horrid land from where nightmares and beauty abide

Kore had always been fond of exploration and her curiosity knew no bounds, it was her weakness and they both knew it, she was helpless to refuse

instead of the silken clad beings, Pluto himself stood at the door, clad in his ebony armor but mercifully without his helm, looking apprehensive and uncomfortable

he looked at the verge of speaking but hints of red burned his cheeks and quickly looked away, she took the unspoken compliment and briefly, her discomfort faded

with a wave of his hand a fissure opened in the wall and he bade her walk through, they stepped from the great castle onto a normal looking street

this was the Asphodel Meadows, the place where ordinary souls go after death, a bustling city in shades of grey, filled with souls going about, but lifeless and devoid as they strode down the street, Pluto pointed out certain souls and told their tale, most of the shades cringed away from his presence, both fearful and obedient

the buildings grew older, the images less distinct, as if the memory of them grew foggy, vague human like shapes instead of the more distinct images where they entered

a large building stood before them and Pluto held the door for her, biding her enter, inside an almost warm glow lit the room, and a lone man sat waiting

Pluto nodded at the man who bowed deeply to both of them before taking out a lyre, Kore would never be able to recall the words but would never forget the emotion

they sat facing the bard, Orpheus, as he sang, tears streaming down her face, an ache like a dagger of ice at the beauty of the music, she saw the tears on Pluto's cheeks as well

without realizing it, in this singular moment she had reached out and as Orpheus sang, they held hands and sobbed together, taken on the journey of a master

once she realized it she quickly took her hand back, shattering the spell of the music and causing the first off note of the show, embarrassed and upset she quickly stood

Orpheus looked afraid for his afterlife, as Pluto seemed to swell in displeasure, his lyre hit the floor as Pluto strode towards him, his anger clear and sharp

please stop, it was me not him that ruined the mood, if you must punish someone let it be me Lord Pluto, his only crime was singing too beautifully and pure

Pluto stopped his march towards Orpheus and faced her, anger at first, but as he looked at her and her fear, sorrow and discomfort, he turned to Orpheus and thanked him

Orpheus thanked her profusely, and bowed so low his head touched the floor before Pluto's boots and gave his most profound thank you before scurrying out

*for you my dream, any time you would like to hear his songs
just ask and it shall be done, he shall be your personal bard,
the Queen's chosen songsmith and poet*

*forgive my displeasure, I thought he had done something to
upset you, this is a realm of rules and they must be followed,
my, our, kingdom is not one of chaos*

*agree to meet again soon and I shall take you to a new part
of our realm, I promise to show you a wondrous time, there is
so much to see in a place so vast*

she could see the hope in his eyes, remember the tears on
his cheek, but that rage stayed barely restrained and frightened her, always a flash or hint of it in every look

but a softness as well when he looked her way, as infre-
quent as such looks were, she could feel the burning in his
lavender orbs, a different barely restrained look

she agreed, a bit more excitedly than she hoped to, and he
opened a portal in the wall and they were quickly back in the
castle again, he opened her door for her

as she entered he grabbed her hand and quickly brought
it to his lips, electrifying and chilled, tingles raced through
her, as she sat feeling the kiss echo she ate another seed

true to his word, Pluto sent Orpheus to visit and entertain
her, and she found herself using the time to learn all she
could about this Realm and the curious God in charge

Orpheus recited the great Battle between Titans and
Olympians, of Kronos castrating Uranus and his blood and
seed creating the giants, of tricky Gaia

a final prophecy from Uranus to Kronos, telling that as he
slew his father so would his children rise up and defeat him,
turning the new king into a tyrant

as Rhea birthed his children, Kronos grabbed and ate
them, leaving nothing to chance, Rhea could bare no more
and replaced Zeus with a rock in a blanket

hidden in a cave and taught the powers of his godhood, Zeus came back and in disguise became the royal cup bearer, pouring mustard into Kronos' wine

the more he consumed the more upset his stomach became until out of his control he began vomiting and released his trapped children to join Zeus

ten years they battled for control of existence, the three brothers, Zeus, Neptune and Pluto led the Olympians to victory, the Titans chained and left to Tartarus

Zeus chose the sky as his kingdom, to lead man and the gods, Neptune chose the sea to have dominion over, Pluto was given the Underworld, the dead now his to rule

given no choice, he used his strongest weapon, his mind, to forge the laws of the Underworld, to lay order and hand down punishments, but he was ever alone

feared by mortals, cast to the Underworld by family, he grew melancholy and angry, while his family played in the warmth he was left in the dark

the gorgons crafted an eye for him, one that allowed him to view the land of the living as he grew more withdrawn, a way to see the other lands from his self perceived cage

Pluto spent his time creating his kingdom, putting order to the chaos, judging the souls of the dead and placing them appropriately, all while watching the world

one day he was alone, slumped down in his throne, pensive and filled with gloom, all the time in the ever dark of his kingdom slowly sapping the joy from his heart

then a vision of beauty filled the room, for it was the first time he had ever spied Kore plucking flowers and playing in the surf with Minerva and Diana

upon that very first glance he felt something new take hold, the desperate loneliness that has been worn like a cloak became too heavy as he saw her face he found himself watching her as she planted the seeds and sent nurturing love into the soil, he set his hand upon the Earth and could feel the vibration of it radiate into him

the dark Lord of the Dead, feared and never mentioned was smitten, fallen for this fair maiden, his disused and atrophied heart began to beat and ache again

he became obsessed, longed to reach out and touch this epic work of perfection, but fear and too much time alone made him doubt his own strength so he went to Zeus

Zeus thought it was hilarious, what need did a god have for love, if a god wanted something he was to take it, for this was the natural way of things on Olympus

he told Pluto if she was his desire than her hand in marriage was his, a simple boon asked and granted, for Pluto never asked for things from his brothers

he encouraged Pluto to go to her then, to sweep her away and take her to his kingdom, this was destined to be for the Underworld needed a queen and a god deserved a mate

Orpheus and Kore talked for days, until an understanding was found, Pluto was a tragic figure that was led the wrong way, but what other way does Zeus know

Kore's time alone down here had shown her desolate sadness in the short period, she could not imagine how it would build over centuries, sullen and all

something in her mind clicked as understanding blossomed, they were both trapped, neither by their own design, she sat pensively and ate another seed and thought

a knock on her door stirred her from her thoughts, Kore had been lost the last few days, her prison, her suitor, the words of Orpheus, all turning over and again

Pluto stood, armor absorbing the candlelight in the doorway, the same inquisitive look on his pale face, eyes fixated and saying more than words could ever convey she felt her face flush at his visage, a tremor in her hands, butterflies dancing in her belly, but the stabbing pain of sorrow flavoring it, adding a dimension to it

Kore, you seem lost today my love, maybe a walk through the caverns will clear your mind, there is beauty to rival even you in the dark depths, none living have ever seen

she nodded, the immensity of the Underworld weighing heavy on her shoulders, together they walked through the castle, past cathedrals and faceless servants

lichen glowed from the walls, luminescent and giving a faint green tinge to the winding caves, water dripping from limestone stalactites, fungi and minerals

they reached a large cavern, empty and circular, at least fifty feet in diameter, empty and dark, so unlike the world above, her home, driving her to her knees

he longed to reach out to her, to alleviate her pain, shower her with the love that filled his every thought, to hold her tight and protect her from everything bad

but he held back and asked her to close her eyes and describe the one place she missed the most of the surface world, to share her personal haven with him

she wanted to fight him, to turn from his tender words, the obvious love in his eyes, but she was unable, his words coaxing a plateau from her mind and heart

she described the field of her childhood, the grass high and soft beneath her toes, the smells of the trees and flowers, the sunlight falling through the leaves

she described her favorite flowers, the lilies and roses, the sweet drooping daffodils and tulips, the romping animals and playful nymphs and satyrs

the sweet touch of the warm southern wind on her cheeks, the gentle rains, the sounds of leaves rustling and taste of nectar, all of it pouring from her, her secret garden finally he asked her to open her eyes, she froze in shock, the cave had become a reproduction of her favorite place, gems and metals formed into her words and thoughts

a large yellow diamond representing Helios off center in the ceiling, lichen casting its glow through its facets, shining down on silver trunked trees with rubies for apples

amethyst blossoms on gentle golden stems, copper laden aquamarine blooms and garnet roses sprang from the floor around her, Pluto, eyes closed stood hands dancing

pale white diamonds twinkled from the ceiling, the stars coming to life on the rocky sky, the constellations winking in the dancing candle as she turned to see it all

she was awestruck by the sheer magnificence of the act, the once empty cave now alive with treasure grown into art, the riches of the ground made two fold real

tears fell, joyful and tinged with sadness, appreciation and ache swirling together as she watched him bring this world to life for her, as he sought to comfort her

she didn't know why she did it, but as if moving on her own she found herself next to mighty Pluto as he crafted, and her lips found his cheek

as she whispered thank you

he froze at this contact, unable or unwilling to move, to break the moment and as her lips touched his for the briefest moment, the sweetest time, he smiled

they stood silent, this singular instance forever scribed into their being and he removed a gauntlet and took her hand into his own, together in her new favorite place

he opened a doorway to this secret garden and locked it in place to open into her suite, sealing the cavern from the caves and making it only for her, his love

bowing deeply, he turned and vanished, leaving her to tend the flowers and watch the stars, as close to above as this strange land could give to her, nearly home tired and overwhelmed by the events of the day she returned to her bed, staring into space and remembering his face as he brought her words to life, the smile as he worked

she sat smiling as well, looking at the invaluable works of art, the gentle scentless flowers grown from her heart and by his hand, absently she popped another seed into her mouth

something changed between Kore and Pluto after their last outing, the door on her room was no longer locked and Orpheus was given a room down the hall from her

for her entire stay she had ignored his invitations to dinner, choosing to stay in her room and then in her private garden, where she could almost pretend she was free

tonight as the servant came to the door, the futile gesture to join the evening feast, she was ready, dressed in a long silken dress of the deepest lavender, amethyst in her hair

as she walked into the great hall the sound of a goblet hitting the floor greeted her as Lord Pluto rose in shock, he stammered a greeting clearly lost in her

she blushed and curtsied low, he rushed to take her hand and kiss it gently, the cool flush of his lips and her heightened pulse a heady combination

she sat and they exchanged pleasantries, still unwilling to imbibe on the offerings of the Underworld, he gave no sign of distress or offense, it was pleasant

long after the food was cleared they sat talking, of the gods and gossip, of simple nothings, enjoying the time together, defenseless and without airs, happy and pure

in an effort to extend this precious time, he suggested they take a stroll, eager as well she agreed and took his offered arm, he gestured at the wall and a door opened

and onto an open field they stepped, wind blowing and rippling the tall grass, Kore dropped to her knees and relished in the feel of the grass, the call of the seeds he explained that this was Elysium, the great Elysian Fields, both part of the Underworld and separate, under their domain and not, the land of heroes and demigods

our role here is less defined as these are the souls of oath keepers and the great, fallen gods and mighty kings, the venerated and wise, and also where my mother resides

they strode across the plains, stopping to converse with the occasional well wisher, praise given to the Lord and Lady of the Dead, and to engage in the occasional debate

she felt out of sorts as it seemed some of these souls knew her, or at least of her, it seemed the great Pluto had come to talk of unrequited love with true philosophers

she found it endearing, slightly embarrassing, and thoroughly enchanting, missing great chunks of conversation as she stared at the pale god alongside her

finally they arrived at a great tree, the largest she had ever seen, and nestled in the trunk grew a great throne in which sat the most beautiful woman she had ever seen

at the sight of them she burst up from her seat and rushed to them, wrapping Pluto into a hug and spinning him off the ground before putting a wary eye on Kore

this is the one who has stolen your heart, the beautiful and perfect Kore of which you endlessly prattle, your muse and desire, instead of following your brother's example

look me in the eye thief, show me this soul capable of enslaving my favorite son, look me in the eye and show me your every secret, your every dark thought

Pluto begged her to stop, for Kore to ignore her tauntings but it was too late, their eyes were locked as one, unblinking and unfocused, he was powerless

an instant, forever and miniscule, stretching on and over in a blink occurred, then it was done, and they fell into an embrace, sobbing and clutching each other *my son, you have made a grave mistake choosing this one, she is fierce and amazing and your equal in every way, she will challenge and perplex, she is as perfect as you said*

Kore, I know this is all confusing and impossible to grasp, and if you choose to love my son know you will be forever changed, the old Kore will cease to exist

but also know his love for you is pure and true, he will be the source of your greatest love and your greatest sorrow, together you can fulfill your greatest dreams at a cost

they spoke for a while after but the air seemed heavy, the mood had shifted subtly and all seemed ready for time alone and they hugged and promised to meet again

they spoke no more as they walked back through the plains, both withdrawn, the words of Rhea haunting their every thought, weighing them down

they parted at her door, she gently kissed his cheek and he her hand, no words spoken or needed, his love an open secret, her feelings murky and ill defined as yet

she sat on her bed and absently twirled her hair, thinking of the words of Rhea, of true love and sacrifice, she placed a seed in her mouth and heard the secret whisper

Kore, the you that came here is dead, from here on you have become someone else, something more, this is your sorrow and dread, but you have become greater

the highs and lows of their last outing cast a pall over everything, the dinner invitations went unanswered, and a heavy melancholy filled the songs Orpheus played

even her garden was no solace from these dark feelings, Rhea's words played over and again through Kore's mind, ill tidings and musings ever at the forefront

the morose atmosphere continued, Pluto barely had a presence in the keep, the silent silken clad creatures stood motionless, this dread filling every soul in Hades then one morning according to the diamond Helios a knock came upon her door, she leapt up, excited for an end to this gloom and doom, he stood stoically, reserved in full armor

she was disappointed by this appearance, his defensive posture, dismayed as he presented her with an ivory set of mail, like his but feminine and a stark counterpoint as well

we hold court this day my love, the last aspect of this domain, the judgement of the truly heinous, their crimes deserving of unending torture in the realm of Tartarus

in everything there must be balance, the Asphodel Meadows is where those who lived normal lives reside, Elysium for the honored fallen, and

Tartarus for the worst of monsters

this darker aspect is one my brothers take great joy in, but I have never had the taste for pain, this is necessary though, for in all things there should be honor and law

she dressed quickly, the armor fitting her perfectly, a gift from Vulcan himself she learned, like a second skin it lay upon her and as she lowered the faceless helm she felt oddly whole

he extended an arm and she took it and they walked through stone to reach the gates of Tartarus, as far beneath Hades as Hades was from Mount Olympus itself

the wailing of the damned filled the acrid air, great demons and monsters chained and tormented lie on all sides of the solitary path through Tartarus to the chamber of judgement

behold Ixion, chained to this flaming wheel, winged and destined to forever fly and spin and burn, like the lust he let rule his life, so much that he dare try and seduce Hera

there is Sisyphus, supposedly so clever he tricked Zeus, now destined to push this boulder up this slope until he can finally place it on top, but lo this boulder has other plans

Tantalum stands there in that pool of water, under the branches of that pear tree, as he reaches for the fruit the branches raise and if he tries to drink the water shall recede, his avarice

she watched the boulder nearly top the hill, only to roll back down a different side, the wheel spinning in the sky, and the frustrations of man denied sustenance so near

she had heard the tales of these men, knew the sins against god and man they had committed, but to see such torment gave a gravity to the tales, it was hard to watch

she understood the faceless helm now, they allowed horror to reach the eyes but no one could tell, it allowed gentle Pluto to be able to witness this torment and remain strong

she gripped his arm tighter and they made their way into the chamber of judgement, where the souls Minos determined needed punishment were placed for sentencing

in the center of the room stood an obsidian throne, polished and jagged, personifying solemn and the gravitas of law and damnation, Pluto stopped and gestured at the throne

as Kore watched an identical throne grew from the floor, the black glass growing and cutting reality it seemed, as it formed a mirror image, Pluto gestured and they sat

a stream of souls came in and they silently listened to the crimes, Pluto, experienced, doled out penance equal to the crime, some simple and others intricate and fitting

she watched, in awe of his ability to sit in judgement, to be able to immediately hold them liable for their sins and accountable for eternity, he was cold and calculating

she was both horrified and understanding, these wretches spent their lives enamored by their own hubris, unable to separate hunger from propriety

Pluto sat rigid and passed judgement on every soul, compassionless and just, an unappetizing part of his role, but one he assumed out of necessity, no pleasure taken

they returned to the great hall as the last cretin was sentenced, the chains of duty weighing heavy this day, she returned to her room to remove the armor and stench of Tartarus the familiar knock of invite to dinner came and she chose to ignore it, lost in what had transpired this day, a pomegranate seed between her teeth, swallowed without thought

the knock came again and she ignored it, sitting on the floor, surrounded by peridot ivy and glittering sapphire azaleas, this strange feeling of understanding in her guts

again the knock and she rose in anger, her thoughts scrambled, she opened the door to find Mercury, winged sandals and helm and a foolish lopsided grin

Kore, Zeus sent me to fetch you, your mother is awfully worried and things haven't been so good with you gone, Pluto knows I am here and will not stand against me, come we leave now

she sat in shock, the rescue she had prayed for finally come, an end to her imprisonment, but now she was unsure, her time had shown her that she had changed

she stood, uncertain and torn, Pluto stood beyond the door, head hung and sorrow written plainly across his face, she tried to meet his eyes but he turned and walked away

Mercury reached out and took her hand, she looked about to speak as the world shifted and she found herself yet again taken from where she wanted to be and thrust out anew

the blinding light, after so long in the darkness was pain, knives in her eyes, she blinked back tears, held down sobs and stood with her back straight, unwilling to show weakness

slowly the world came into focus and she found herself standing on Mount Olympus, the entire host of gods and goddesses in a ring around her, she looked each in the eye

but there was no thanks in that look, disdain colored her impression of them, Orpheus sang of their games and spoiled lives, Pluto taught her the gods should be noble

Zeus seemed smug as he led Demeter to her, as if all of this was not at least partially his fault, her mother pulled her in and placed her into a crushing embrace, tears flowed freely

but Kore scanned all over, looking for the one face she
knew would not be there, so she looked for where she hoped
he was watching and gave a strong smile, private and his

the gods spoke over one another, Demeter demanding
Pluto be punished for this, the gods demanding that life be
given back to the soil, a deal was made and must be honored

Kore listened to the tale of her mother's rage and sorrow,
of the blanket of cold that had covered the land the last six
months, of death and starvation

she was shocked, all of this was too much, her mother,
venerated and loved had come to show she was just as selfish
as the others, her sorrow more important than the rest

they could see this was too much too quickly, and after
checking to make sure she was fine, that he had not been
untoward, or tried to trick her with food or wine

she barely spoke, her every wish granted, returned home,
no longer imprisoned in the land of the dead, this should be
the happiest moment of the last half year

but flashes of lavender at the edge of her sight, the cool
pale skin, a tingle on her hand from where those lips had
lain, the chills that raced through her at his touch

the oracles exclaimed delight as the shows receded, the
land itself began to thaw as Demeter returned her passion
and held her daughter, the gods cheered as a warm wind blew

Diana and Minerva clutched her close, a celebration on
the hallowed mount, ambrosia and honeyed mead flowed
and all took up goblets but two, Venus and Kore

Venus had not stopped staring at Kore, head cocked and
searching her eyes, a sly smile on her face as she saw what she
sought, a subtle head nod and a secret was known to both

Venus leaned in, her beauty intoxicating to all who beheld
it, her hair like spun gold, each strand seemingly with life of
its own, her perfume perfection

you know your mother will never let you go back to him, your
shadowed love, she will let humanity die and ice take over the
world, her darling Kore, she cannot stand to be apart

yet the Styx and Lethe overflow as he weeps for his lost love,
the damned sing a song of loss for their heart broken master,
clouds even cover the Elysian Fields in darkness

Rhea spoke to me and bade me remind you of her words to
you and asked me to give you this boon, she said you would
understand, it seems Pluto has really gotten to you my dear

she giggled, the sound of tinkling bells, and walked away,
Kore looked down at the boon from Rhea, wrapped in black
lace lay the pomegranate from her room

the party grew louder, the tales more grandiose, of battles
and conquests, and the cheers from below echoed as well,
the ground grew malleable and soon seeds were nestled safely

but Kore sat, staring at the pomegranate and replaying
Rhea's words, she could not imagine a worse sorrow than
being separated from the one she now knew she loves

the air of seriousness, of obligation that weighed on his
shoulders, the alienation from his family, the pressure of
duty and honor that made up his ebony mail

but also the clever wordplay, the beauty of her garden
made with his own hands, how he could not maintain her
gaze without blushing, the lavender longing

she realized too late and now torn by her duty and obligation she felt cut by a thousand daggers, and understood him
even more, as a sheen of ice began to grow inside of her

Kore walked amongst the revelers, smiling and thanking
them for their well wishes, eyes searching the crowd until
she found her target, Mercury through his staff, Caduceus

the twin serpents entwined upon the staff, hissing at any
who strayed too closely and occasionally at the wings of his
helm as well, drew her to him and she gently drew him aside

Lord Mercury, I never got a chance to thank you in the rush to get back to Olympus, your speed and grace are that of legend and you have my most sincere thanks

but I also need ask a favor my Lord, a small boon but precious and important to me and must be done now, can you take a letter to Hades for me and deliver it to Pluto himself

she blushed and shyly held out the scroll, wrapped tight with a knot of her own hair, a P the only adornment visible, which he quickly grabbed and tucked into his bag

with a wink and nod of his helm he was gone, and just as quickly back again as if he never left, a gentle pat on her shoulder and he walked away, absorbed into the crowd

she hoped he understood, that this is what has to be done, his pride and arrogance the largest flaw in her plan, but she realized duty comes first, a lesson learned from him

stepping up to the dais, Kore cleared her throat and gathered the attention of the party to herself, the chill in her growing, filling her with purpose and an emerging power

Lord Zeus, gods and goddesses of Olympus, we have all gathered to give thanks for my safe return and the green of spring from this long winter, but one is not here

I ask that you call Lord Pluto from Hades to join us, there is an important matter I fear we must all speak of, of such urgency I fear it must be addressed immediately

she stood, head slightly bowed as a murmur swept the crowd, Demeter stood and come forth, alarm and confusion on her face, Zeus nodded and signaled Mercury

her heart thundered in her chest as time seemed to pause, mere seconds passed but it felt infinitely stretched out until he stood before her, his familiar scent of hemlock wafting

they met each other's eyes and another infinite moment occurred before a slap like lightning rung as Demeter struck him, his head reeled and a red hand shone in his cheek quickly the closest to her restrained her, and Pluto did nothing but clasp his hands behind his back, as if nothing had happened at all and faced Zeus

Zeus shrugged and pointed at Kore, this was none of his doing and he so wanted to enjoy the spectacle playing out in front if him, the gods were overly fond of drama

I summoned you my Lord, for there has been a great injustice performed upon me, all have sought to tell me how to live my life, you seeking to make me your queen is first

but you Mother, you have taken the whole world hostage with your actions, let all of mankind suffer in your grief, your refusal to see reason has brought us here, taking me away

well we shall have to have a compromise, for I have told you all a lie, Pluto did trick me, while we were in his palace he convinced me to eat six pomegranate seeds

we all know what this means, if you eat anything of the Underworld you are destined to remain there forever, I was weak and he took advantage of me, I never stood a chance

she tried to speak with her eyes to Pluto but her words shredded him, she saw the pain at her accusal, the slump of his shoulders at her words left him nearly limp

frantic talk erupted and Demeter swooned in the arms of those restraining her, Zeus hid his amusement behind a facade of dismay and anger

the party was immediately over, the minor gods and demigods hurriedly drained goblets and tankards and rushed out of the area, soon only a handful of gods remained

is this true brother, did you indeed trick her into eating pomegranate seeds in your realm, knowing the full consequences of this action, that she would remain trapped

Pluto looked around the remaining faces and then only into Kore's and nodded yes one time, his eyes imploring hers, but she let the ice fill her being and just stared back the gods and goddesses stared at Pluto in dismay, they had just calmed Demeter into allowing the world to thaw and become lovely again now this new treachery

my lords and ladies, I apologize for my error but in what way is having your soon to be wife eat of her realm, why would I not want her to be part of my life until the end of days

allow me to make a suggestion, a compromise of sorts, since Kore ate six seeds in my realm then she must stay by my side six months of the year, as my wife and co-ruler

Demeter exploded at this, but the rest of the room ignored her, Pluto's words finding purchase in their minds, if he was willing to make amends there was no reason to dismiss him

but what of humanity, this first freezing nearly destroyed them, Demeter's refusal to agree left them alone for half the year and this would render them all obsolete

again I may be able to help, one of my duties is domain over rebirth, have man build great silos to store their grains and mark them with my symbol and I will keep them viable

the assembly listened and found this satisfactory, yet still Demeter raged and swore she would not abide by this, she called it a mockery and leapt at Pluto again

another thunderous slap was heard, this time Demeter held her face and stared in shock at Kore, her daughter stood tall and proud in her face, the entire room froze

enough, enough of this petulant rage, do you not see the length Pluto is willing to go to make everyone happy, the length I am willing to go to keep mankind and god content

I am grown Mother, a goddess in my own right and will live my life as I see fit, not the obedient daughter or wife, but as my own personification, not beholden to any but myself

I accept your terms Lord Pluto, to rule by your side as your queen half the year and to live above planting seeds and helping the crops the other, a goddess of two realms but know the Kore that both of you have loved is no more, she has died and I have risen from the husk, I have accepted my duty and shall now be known as Persephone

with that she stepped forward and kissed Pluto in front of the assembled host, and a great applause roared but neither of them heard any of it, lost in each other and blissfully in love

when they separated another roar erupted and Pluto stood breathless and flushed crimson, and Kore, nay, Persephone embraced her mother and whispered her love

Pluto bowed to his future mother in law and bade her welcome in their realm, extending an offer to visit Rhea in Elysium to start planning the wedding soon to occur

and a great change was felt throughout the realms of man and god, gone were the endless days of summer and endless bountiful harvests

on the day Persephone travels to rule Hades with her doting husband Pluto, the green begins to fade to brown and the winds turn chill from the North as Demeter sleeps in her bed

soon the leaves change color and are shed as the blanketing snows come, but mankind learns to adapt and store excess goods for these seasons with thanks to the Underworld blessing

and in Hades the hall brightens and Orpheus regales all with tales of beast and man, of heroes and legend, while Persephone and Pluto rule side by side and hand in hand

all celebrate the day of her return, when the trees begin to grow blossoms and the life flows back into the Earth, Persephone planting fields of lavender and sowing seeds

they work the fields and bask in the warmth as she and Demeter reunite, the animals and man growing fat in the long days, even the gods come to the land to play

and all tell the tale of Kore who took Pluto's heart and how he stole hers in return, of his trickery and her will, of the newly formed seasons and of Persephone, Queen of the Dead in Hades - *my dearest Persephone, you know that the pomegranate was a gift from Gaia, never once did I try and trick you, I was after your heart, unfettered and freely given*

yes my love, but I could think of nothing else and your mother sent me that pomegranate and it was all I could do, I apologize for my deception but all I wanted was to be with you

a chuckle, then a kiss

the end

March 15th

The clock ticked to five thirty. My phone lit up and Spotify started up. The opening notes of some Foo Fighters song began and I opened my eyes. Immediately I can see his face. I don't look over for his still sleeping body because I know he isn't going to be there. Not ever again. We were finished. For good this time. The finality of the last fight, the things said in anger. The things said in truth. It was done.

And I was left with an ache that no bubble gum pop song could ever fill.

I didn't even need the alarm today. I knew my state of mind. I had called my boss last night and said I had the flu. I was going to be near worthless if I went to the office. I made coffee and sat on the couch. All around the living room were mementos of us. Pictures on the wall, that stupid vase he had to have on the shelf, and his coat on the chair. I hated myself for doing it but I grabbed the coat and put it on. Tears rolling down my cheek as I sat there smelling him and replaying his words. The jagged edges of my broken heart rubbing the inside of chest raw with every heaving breath.

I hated feeling this way. Hated myself for letting him get so deeply into the fabric of my being. I stood and grabbed that ugly fucking vase and threw it against the wall. The shattering felt good in its own petty way. Fuck you and your vase. And your space. And feeling like you were being smothered you self righteous son of a bitch. Fuck you.

I grabbed a bottle of whiskey and a book of poetry and went back to bed. Alternating between long pulls of the burning liquid and verses of sorrow. When the whiskey was gone I grabbed the wine. When the wine was gone I grabbed the vodka from the freezer. And when the vodka was gone so was I. The sun had vanished like feeling in my face. I couldn't see through the double vision and tears. An odd sense of calm fell over my overly inebriated brain. And then I passed out. My last move was to make sure I was on my back in case I got sick. I didn't want to wake up in the morning.

———

The clock ticked to five thirty. My phone lit up and Spotify started up. The opening notes of some Foo Fighters song began and I opened my eyes. The ache greeted me and surprisingly no hangover. That was nice at least. I'm really not a drinker and the amount I drank yesterday could have put me in the hospital.

I got up and went to the kitchen and made coffee. As it percolates I fire up the computer. The solid state drive he installed for me is a miracle. Fifteen seconds from power up to ready. If everything could be that speedy and reliable. The disappointment is palpable when all I have in my inbox is offers for boner pills and dating sites. I thought maybe he would have...

It is stupid. Over means over. He is stubborn as hell and when he puts his mind to something he means it. The smell of the coffee calls to me and I pour that first mug of black electricity. As I carry it back into the living room I nearly burn myself as it falls from my numb fingers. The vase. That ugly fucking vase is sitting on the end table mocking me. I know I threw it against the wall yesterday. I have the cut on my pinkie from when I...

The cut is gone.

I run into the kitchen and look on the counter. The whiskey bottle sits unopened. The freezer has the vodka. The wine sits on the cupboard.

Was it all a dream? Did I make it all up? I grab my phone. March 15th. Thursday. Today should be Friday by my reckoning. We went to dinner on Wednesday and he ended it. The fourteenth. It is burned into my brain because Saturday, is St Patrick's day and we had plans to go to the parade on Greenville. I guess my mind is playing tricks on me.

I finish the pot of coffee, every last drop of it, while scrolling through the gallery on my phone. The last two years of my life. Of our life. Trips to the zoo, the museum, that shitty Mexican restaurant he loves with the lights and train that runs around the entire place. His birthday party where he finally introduced me to his parents. The cruise to Alaska to see the glaciers. Every bit of the last two years revolved around him.

And he needed a break. I am exhausting. Too needy. Too clingy. Too in love and it is smothering.

Fuck him. Or at least that is what I want to think. I can't quite make myself. Like deleting the pics of us. I can't quite bring myself to hit the button. Because then it is over. Really over. Not the maybe he does need a break and will come back when he realizes the mistake he made kind of over I am clinging to right now.

But for real over.

I hate myself as I open Facebook and look at his profile. Check his status. It's complicated. What the fuck is that supposed to mean? It's complicated. It damn well wasn't complicated when he tore my heart out and pissed all over it. How he did it in a public place so I couldn't freak out. So I had to choke down the bile and tears and not make a spectacle of myself. That was not complicated. That was premeditated.

Premeditated murder.

And who the fuck is this liking all of his updates all of a sudden? Who the fuck is this vulture swooping in?

I would throw my phone against the wall. Shatter it. Break it into as many pieces as my psyche is. But what if he tries to call? If I don't answer right away maybe he will not come back.

I set it down. Upside down so I don't have the urge to pick it back up. Which I immediately do. Just to make sure the ringer is on in case someone calls. Not him. But someone. It is. To be sure I send myself a text. It comes through with a bell toll. Just making sure the phone works.

I am pathetic. No wonder he left.

The next couple hours is spent cleaning. Dusting. Vacuuming. Dishes. I cleaned the windows. Made the bed. Idle hands are the devil's plaything. Idle thoughts are the devil's curse. The house is immaculate. I turn on the television and scroll through the DVR. I cannot watch any of this. We watch these shows together. He would hate it if I was ahead of him. I scroll through everything twice and nothing sounds as good as laying with him and watching the ceiling fan spin.

That whiskey is still in the kitchen.

Somehow I am now sobbing and drinking. First the whiskey. Then the vodka. Then it is later than it should be and my phone hasn't rang once. No new messages for the three hundredth time. I decide to go to bed and trip over the corner of the coffee table. I feel my nose crunch but in that third person experience that only the truly shitfaced do. I staggered to the bed as blood flows down my face. As tears stream down my cheeks.

Nothing matters. Nothing fucking matters at all.

The clock ticked to five thirty. My phone lit up and Spotify started up. The opening notes of some Foo Fighters song began and I opened my eyes. I hate this fucking song.

I stagger to the bathroom to see how bad my face looks. Besides purple rings like a neon raccoon my face is fine. I could use a shave. The stubble on my head is showing. I don't understand. I go back and grab my phone off the dock. March 15th. What the fuck.

The house is a mess. The whiskey is unopened on the counter. It is Thursday. Again.

That Bill Murray movie; I am living that movie. *Groundhog Day*.

I open my phone and press his name. Straight to voicemail. I try again fifteen times. Send him a text saying it is important. I am freaking out. Is this really happening? Am I caught in a loop?

I turn on the television and go to On Demand. Nothing. Netflix. There. I watch the movie I may or may not be living. Two hours later I have no more answers than I had before. Unless I want to learn piano and kidnap a rodent that was a waste of time.

I try and call him again but it still goes to voicemail. I leave a series of increasingly frantic messages. And texts. He doesn't respond at all. I open the whiskey. And a bottle of Tylenol PM. I do shots to swallow the pills. In a little under three hours I have consumed all one hundred pills and the entire bottle. I can barely keep my eyes open. The last image I have is the no new message screen.

The clock ticked to five thirty. My phone lit up and Spotify started up. The opening notes of some Foo Fighters song began and I opened my eyes.

Not again. March 15th. Thursday.

I get dressed and wait for eight to roll around. I get in the car and drive to his house. He leaves at eight fifteen on the dot. Punctual as this waking nightmare. I stand outside the door of his building waiting for him. When eight thirty hits I realize he is not coming down.

I call his phone but it goes straight to voicemail. I try his parents but they don't answer either.

I can feel my mind breaking as I try and wrap it around what is happening. I return to my car and drive towards home while I try his line over and over again. I don't see the light turn red. Or the delivery truck. The impact of the steering wheel against my chest is the first sign of something going wrong.

The clock ticked to five thirty. My phone lit up and Spotify started up. The opening notes of some Foo Fighters song began and I opened my eyes.

I cannot do this again.

I grab the toaster from the kitchen and plug it in as I draw a nice hot bath. I step into the tub and knock the toaster in with me. The smell of burning hair fills the room as the lights flicker.

The clock ticked to five thirty. My phone lit up and Spotify started up. The opening notes of some Foo Fighters song began and I opened my eyes.

Fuck.

I go to the window that overlooks the park. Take a running start and feel the glass carve into me as I dive head first through it.

The clock ticked to five thirty. My phone lit up and Spotify started up. The opening notes of some Foo Fighters song began and I opened my eyes.

No. No. No. No. No. No. No. No.

The phone hits the wall. Then the dock. I roam through the house destroying everything I can get my hands on. I am rage. The Tasmanian Devil on meth. At some point in my wanton destruction there is a pounding on the front door. I grab a knife and open it, blood covering my hands and face. It is a cop and I charge him. The impact of three slugs to the chest and my legs give out from under me.

The clock ticked to five thirty. My phone lit up and Spotify started up. The opening notes of some Foo Fighters song began and I opened my eyes.

Stagger into the bathroom and see that same fucking face looking at me. I don't recognize it. Not completely. I begin bashing it into the mirror. It breaks but the enemy just keeps smiling back in a thousand smaller views. I grab the biggest piece and bring it to my throat. As the blood sprays I see a blinking red light from behind the frame.

The clock ticked to five thirty. My phone lit up and Spotify started up. The opening notes of some Foo Fighters song began and I opened my eyes.

Blinking red light. I take deep breaths and try and quell the insanity taking grip on my mind. I go into the bathroom and try and pull the mirror off of the wall but it won't budge. I grab my electric razor and bash it against the fucking thing. Remove the jagged glass in great handfuls, unmindful of the cuts on my fingers.

There is a hole in the wall. And in the hole is a camera. Red blinking light staring back at me.

Is this real?

Have I gone so far down the rabbit hole that I am imagining this? This cycle? This camera?

I do a Google search for if the house is bugged. Turn off all the lights and look for more red lights. I find a device in the vase. A slight green light blinks from the frame of a picture on the wall. Under the couch is another. I tear the apartment apart and find fifteen devices. Shine a flashlight at the mirror in the closet and see something behind it. Tear it down and find another camera.

Someone is watching me. Making me live this eternal cycle of hell. I gather everything and take it to the police station down the street. I wait for hours before a detective is free to talk to me. I try and explain what is happening to him. The last couple days. The last same day over and over. He has me sit in a room while he takes the devices to be analyzed.

Someone else comes into the room. A doctor. They think I am insane. A danger to myself and others. Two more men come in as I start yelling. They hold me down as the doctor administers a shot to my arm. The world gets heavy and I try and explain I am not crazy.

The clock ticked to five thirty. My phone lit up and Spotify started up. The opening notes of some Foo Fighters song began and I opened my eyes.

I am alone. I don't leave my bed. No noise. They are watching me. Waiting for me to make a move. I won't. I refuse to be their sick twisted fucking entertainment.

I hear them in the walls. Behind the walls. Walking and talking to each other. They are curious as to what my next move will be. What I will do next. I won't give them the satisfaction. Won't give in. They haven't won. They can't break me. I see the light blinking on the dresser. I don't look directly at it. Pretend it isn't there.

I want to die. But that lets them have what they want. And we can't have that. No we cannot. Any sign of weakness and they win. I can stay still all day. Every day.

I just lay there and sing that song about my hero. I can do this forever.

I can do this forever.

The clock ticked to five thirty. My phone lit up and Spotify started up. The opening notes of some Foo Fighters song began and I kept my eyes closed. Just let the song play.

WINDOWS

"Need some help?" a voice said from behind the headlights of the fifty seven Cadillac. A cherry red beast with fins on the back, chrome and style radiating off of it in nearly palpable waves. A real beauty with curves to match.

Ed stood silent for a moment as if weighing his answer carefully. His Chevy was stuck in the muddy grass on the side of the gravel road by the creek. For the last hour he had been gathering wood to place under the tires in an effort to gain some traction from the sinking saturated soil. He had nearly reached the end of his patience when he heard the sounds of the Caddy on the quiet country lane. At first he thought he imagined it over the sound of his tires digging deeper and deeper into the muck. A smile broke across his fury as he turned and shielded his eyes from the light and stepped out of his car.

"That would be great. I'd appreciate it mightily," he replied. "Got a rope?"

The figure stepped from behind the open door and into the light, a teenage guy with a blonde buzz cut and the remnants of acne on his cheeks. His varsity jacket spotless and the large white A stood out against the red fabric.

"I have something better," he answered with a smile and walked back to the trunk. A couple seconds later he returned with the clanking of chains and a big grin. "Name's Bartholomew, Bart really. That's my girlfriend Bella in the car."

Ed squinted into the light and could make out a vague shape waving from the passenger seat. He smiled and waved back. "I'm Ed, and over there," he pointed over by the creek where a shape was sitting against a tree, "is my girl Melody." He stuck out his hand and received a firm handshake from Bart.

"Nice to meet you sir. Looks like you got in pretty deep there. The rains the last week have had the creek overflowing."

Ed shook his head in embarrassment. "Mel and I took a wrong turn and stopped to check the map and then we kind if started to..."

"Watched the stars?" Bart filled in with a knowing smirk.

"Yes indeed! We're not from around here and not all that used to the country life."

"City folk huh. Where you guys from?" Bart asked politely as he wrapped the chain around his bumper and passed the other end to Ed.

"Up North, Madison area. Thank you again Bart, I was about to start walking in hopes of finding a farm to ask for help."

"You would have been in for a hike, the nearest farm to here is about fifteen miles that way," he said pointing back the direction he had come from. "She lives another twenty that way." He pointed in the opposite direction.

"Well then I must be doubly lucky you happened upon us."

"It's nothing Ed. Just being neighborly. My dad would have been disappointed had I just kept driving when I saw your brake lights and heard the tires spinning."

"Well he did good," Ed replied tugging the chain to make sure it was secure. "Seems good, ready to try this?"

"Sure am."

Bart and Ed got in their vehicles and in a matter of minutes the Chevy was on dry land again. Ed jumped out and began removing the chains and passed then back. The sounds of the cicadas roaring in the night around them. Bella also got out, carefully avoiding the mud in her saddle shoes. She was gorgeous, long brunette hair in a ponytail over one pink cardiganed shoulder; a poodle stitched into her black skirt.

Ed extended his hand and she demurely shook it and blushed as he whistled. "Well aren't you just the prettiest thing?"

Bart finished putting the chain away and came over and put his arm around her shoulder. "That she is. You should have seen her at the dance tonight."

"Bart! Stop it, you're embarrassing me," she said but didn't mean a word of it. He just chuckled and pulled her in a little tighter.

"Well thank you again Bart. It was a blessing you stopped. And you as well Bella. It's getting pretty late, don't want you guys getting in trouble for missing curfew now."

Bella was looking over where Melody was sitting against the tree. "Is she asleep?"

Ed looked chagrined and pulled the empty pint of whiskey from his pocket. "You could say that."

They all laughed for a moment before Bart looked down at his watch. "Golly, it is getting pretty late. You are right. Are you guys going to be okay now?"

"We will be now thanks to you heroes."

"Oh gosh, you're going to give him a big head. It's big enough already, he's Mr. Captain of the football team."

Bart blushed, "And has the most beautiful girl in school as his gal."

She reached up and patted his cheek.

Ed smiled at them. Young love was truly something to behold. "Alright guys, thank you again. And thank your father for me Bart for raising you the right way."

"Will do good luck out there."

They shook hands again and Bart opened Bella's door for her. They waved as they began to pull away.

Ed was relieved. He didn't really know what he was going to do when he realized how deep the car had sunk. He began to walk over to where Melody was sitting against the tree. And that is when Bart chose to pull wide instead of backing up and his headlights shone directly on her serene form. Unfortunately it also highlighted the red stain that had soaked through the front of her white blouse.

"Well damn it," Ed muttered, "you just had to peek."

The Cadillac came to a shuddering sudden stop as Bart slammed on the brakes and shifted hard to park. Ed's shoulders slumped as he reached into the waistband of his jeans and in one fluid motion pulled aimed and shot his Colt twice. Once through each of the teen lovers chests. Anger infusing his entire being as he unloaded again and again into the windshield of the cherry red convertible. When the hammer clicked on an empty chamber for the fifth or sixth time he calmed down enough to relax his position.

"Ain't this just a god damned mess now," he said to the stars.

Could nothing go right? It all had been steadily falling apart on him the last couple days. He shook his head and walked over to the Caddy and surveyed the situation. Bart was making wet sucking sounds as he tried to draw breath and his blood did its best to escape the confines of his body. He placed his hand over Bart's mouth and soon the struggle was over.

"You just had to drive away friend. Could have taken your girl home and maybe snuck a kiss or two and everything would have been just fine," he muttered and shook his head. "Now we find ourselves in a pickle for sure."

He looked around, trying to figure out how to clean this up. His eyes lit up as he saw a large rock on the ground and he knew what to do. He turned the wheel slightly off of its bearing directly at Melody and towards the large oak tree next to the one he had leaned her up against. He placed the rock on the accelerator and moved the shifter to drive as the engine roared, barely getting his arm out as it barreled away. The squeal of metal being compacted by the thick trunk of the old tree and glass shattering filled the night. It was enough to quiet the disharmonic symphony of wildlife. Albeit only for a second but he relished the silence as it blanketed the night.

He walked over and picked up Melody, careful to avoid getting blood on his mud splattered clothes, and dumped her in the backseat. A crimson streak on the white leather interior like an errant swipe of a paint brush as her limp form collapsed on the bench seat. He looked at the remains of the car, Bart's father's he guessed. If he had known it was going to end like this he would have just shot them outside the car and taken it as his own. What a waste of good old Detroit steel this was. He shook his head as he popped open his trunk and grabbed the metal canister of gas and began to pour it on the bodies and across the crumpled hood. He pulled a cigarette out of his pocket and lit it while staring at Bella. Damn waste of a perfectly good woman too he thought shaking his head. The dashboard had done her no favors as one of her eyes had popped directly out of the socket from the crushing impact. He took a long drag on the cigarette, the orange ember flaring as the gas fumes filled the air. One last puff and he casually flicked it onto Melody's lap where it ignited in a fireball that quickly consumed the white leather and three corpses. The blue flames raced over the red metal and once it got to the mangled engine a whoosh as it felt like all the available air was sucked out of the atmosphere. He was nearly knocked to the ground The cicadas had gone silent as the sharp cracks of the gun firing had gone off and just resumed their chorus of the damned as the entire car began spewing black smoke in a thick cloud.

As he drove away he saw flames licking the sky and smiled as he headed towards the farmhouse Bart so helpfully gave directions to. Tonight had not turned out how he had expected it would. First Melody decided she didn't want to keep driving to Mexico with him. She was homesick and missed her parents and sisters. The great adventure beginning to spoil after only three days. He hadn't meant to stab her. He really hadn't. It just sort of happened. One minute she was crying and begging him to turn around. The next he was laying her against the tree. Then the car was stuck and he was about to abandon it and her. Like his mother said between swigs of booze and the cavalcade of different suitors, when God shuts a door he opens a window. Never made much sense to him growing up but now its meaning was crystal clear.

He turned on the radio and some twanging guitars and a reed thin voice came out of the speakers singing about how lonesome he was that he could cry. Ed shook his head and turned it off. All they seemed to play down here was this sappy music. He lit another smoke and let the sound of the wind fill him as he drove. Right on cue a farmhouse about a mile back from the road came into the dark night. He wondered if this was a door or a window as he reached into the glove compartment and removed a box of bullets from beneath a bloody knife. He hoped it was a door but knew it didn't matter.

He had tried to do it the right way. He really had. But best intentions were meaningless if the action didn't match the intent.

When Melody told him she was pregnant he knew he would marry her. Make her an honest woman. It wasn't his fault it all went sideways. She was ecstatic about the baby but equally afraid of her parents' reaction. He suggested they run away like thieves in the night. They could sneak away to Chicago and get themselves set with new lives. Lay low for a while and when things seemed to be cooled off triumphantly return with the precious cargo. But she didn't want to leave that way. Her family was important to her and he respected her decision to be honest with them.

They were less than understanding about the situation. Her father punched him when he asked permission to marry his oldest daughter. The old man's face turned purple with rage that he had the nerve to ask such a stupid question. Ed was not in the same league as Melody. The sinful bastard son of a drunken whore from the bad side of town. Poor white trash with the audacity to try and snag an upper crust wife. Melody screamed at her father to stop after the third hit. Ed just curled in a ball, he had worse beatings from the men who visited his house to spend time with his mother.

Then she finally broke down and told her parents the truth. The blows stopped raining down as shock froze both of her parents in place. Ed made his way to his feet and stood protectively next to Melody. She stiffened as his arm slid around her shoulders and then nearly collapsed as the sobbing began. Her parents said nothing, just stared at each other as their worst fear came true in front of them. Ed was disgusted. These were supposed to be better people, higher class. But they were no better than anyone else he realized. And he had corrupted and ruined their baby girl. He stared daggers at them and spit blood onto the lawn.

They wouldn't even look at her, the shame burning so strongly in their breasts. Her mother, white faced and standing rigid, turned abruptly and walked to the house. Melody, sobbing, begged her to talk to them. But she acted as if she didn't hear a word and climbed to the porch and walked in without a glance back.

Her father stood for a moment longer, eyes on the ground. She pleaded with him to just talk, to understand. He shook his head and spit at her before turning to follow his wife. She pulled free of Ed and followed him to the house, still begging for him to pay attention to her words. And he turned with no expression on his face and slapped her as hard as he could across the cheek before walking in. The click of the lock they seldom ever used echoing in the clear night.

Ed did everything he could to try to comfort her. Every breath sending waves of pain through him as he wrapped his arms around her and tried to not get blood all over her. She just quaked and sobbed into his chest in misery that sent shivers of agony through his body. He just held her though, waiting for the storm to pass. He wanted to tell her they didn't matter, that they would prove them all wrong when they saw how happy their family was. But he stopped knowing she wasn't ready to hear that quite now. In a few days she would see the truth of it all. But for now he just had to be there for her.

The door unlocking was like a gunshot in the empty night and she turned in excitement thinking they had changed their minds. Instead Mel's mother opened the door and set a suitcase on the porch filled with her eldest daughter's possessions.

"Don't come back. Please," she said in a hollow voice before shutting the door and relocking it.

Melody fell to her knees in disbelief. Ed grabbed the bag and put it in the backseat and opened her door for her. He helped her up and guided her into the passenger side to sit down. He got in and started as the engine turned over gently rubbed her knee. Melody just sobbed as they pulled away.

"We don't need them. We'll grab my stuff and head down South. Maybe all the way to Mexico. Get a little plot of land and a couple donkeys. Raise our family away from all the judging eyes of those that never cared about us. It'll be heaven."

She shook her head noncommittally and continued to cry as her entire world crumbled around her. Seventeen and pregnant with a bastard child. What did it matter? Her family tossed her out like the trash she had slept with. Nothing was going to be okay again. She knew it. So she just agreed as a part of her died inside.

"Bobby is working overnight at the motel. We will swing by my mom's and then head there for the night. He'll get us a room to crash in while we make our plans for the road."

His house was a barely standing shack at the edge of town. Overgrown weed ingested lawn and partially standing formerly white picket fence like Stonehenge around it. The garbage can by the side of the road was overflowing with empty glass bottles of the cheap stuff his mother's 'visitors' brought when they came by. And it was a steady stream of men, especially on the weekends.

"Wait here for a second while I explain what's happening to her, okay baby?"

She just stared out the window, not even acknowledging he spoke. He shook his head and got out of the car. The empty driveway was a plus, usually there was someone over. He walked in through the battered screen door and the stale alcohol smell nearly gagged him.

"Ed? Is that you? Bring me my gin you no good bastard!"

"Yes ma'am. Melody is here too, waiting in the car," he replied opening a cupboard door and finding the pint of gin.

"That hussy? She ain't living here! You hear me? That stuck up little whore and her rich family have never done anything but look down on people like us. I told you what would happen if you tried to date a girl from a family like that, didn't I? But you didn't listen to me, never do you ungrateful shit."

"I love her, and she loves me Mom. We are going to start a family together down in Texas or maybe Mexico. Away from all of this..."

"Boy, bring me my gin and shut your fool mouth. She isn't going to stay with a loser like you. Just like your daddy, the good Lord gave you more cock than brains. You hear me? More cock than brains!"

He heard her. She said it all the time to him. Just like his no good idiot daddy that was smart enough to know a dead end when he saw one and left town as quickly as he could. He would be proud to be just like him. He would be better. Better. He didn't even know his father's name. She wouldn't say, or more accurately probably didn't even know. But when she got pregnant it ruined her hopes and dreams. And she had made it her goal to crush any of his in return. Some people weren't born to be parents. Lacked the necessary tools to be able to think about anyone but themselves.

"Yes ma'am."

All his life it was this. Someone trying to take him down. Didn't they realize there is no place lower than the bottom? Than living in the hell of his drunk whore mother spending every penny on gin? The night callers that would rather spit on him than look at him. Or the even worse ones that hit him or tried to do worse. But that was over beginning right now.

No more.

He was done with it. This was the straw that broke the camel's back. He would prove to them all he was not a toy to be battered and abused. He was a man and deserved some respect. He reached under the sink and grabbed the bottle of bleach and carefully poured it into the half empty bottle of gin. Shook it up real nice. He gave a sniff and the bleach smell was just under the surface.

He smiled and took it to her. She didn't even look up at him from her perch at her vanity where she applied a thick coat of foundation, just snarled, "About time. Why does it smell like bleach in here? Did you make another mess? Boy can you do nothing right?"

"Sorry ma'am, I cleaned it up. It was just a little spill."

"You had better have. Start a family? Barely able to take care of yourself and do simple chores for me. Poor baby will probably die of starvation if it has to rely on you as a father. You are worthless boy. Worthless like your daddy."

"Yes Mother. I'm sorry."

She made a noise in her throat at that and unscrewed the cap off the bottle and brought it to her lips. That's when he grabbed her wrist. Forcing the bottle to her lips and pinching her nose shut as the mix poured down her throat. Her eyes widened as she tasted the bleach and she struggled to fight him off. He held her wrist as if made from iron and didn't let go until the last dregs drained out. He slapped her and put his hand over her mouth to keep her from spitting any out. Then he reached over and grabbed one of the silk scarves a caller had given her and wrapped it around her and the back of the chair. She tried to fight back and began yelling incomprehensibly but he was far stronger and bigger than she was. He took the stocking she had ready to wear on the vanity, filled her mouth with one leg and gagged her with the other.

"My no good daddy was a better man than you ever deserved you dried up old whore. You feel that in your guts? I bet it burns. Just like the fires in hell. But I bet you find that out soon enough as well. We're leaving town and you will never see us again."

He watched her struggle against the bonds and smiled. She wasn't going to be able to free herself. She realized it and tried to plead through the makeshift gag. He ignored her and rifled through her jewelry box. He knew the good stuff was at the bottom and happily showed her as he stuffed them into his pockets. Fear and hate fought across her face with hatred eventually winning.

"The bleach won't kill you Momma. Just make you sick as a dog. We're leaving. Tonight. Goodbye and I hope we never see each other again. You hear me? Never again. I'm free. We're free of you and her parents. Free to live our own lives. Our way."

He grabbed his duffel bag, the only thing his no good daddy left him and threw all his clothes into it. Grabbed the coffee tin from on top of the cupboard his mother thought he didn't know about and removed the money she had been hiding. He knew one day she planned on taking it and leaving him in the middle of the night. He had heard her drunkenly talking about it to her sister that lived across town. Buying a bus ticket and going to California to start over. It was a lie and they both knew it. She could never stay sober long enough to see anything through.

He took his bag to the car and

Bella looked at him listlessly. "Are you okay Ed? What happened?" she asked emotionlessly.

"Nothing to worry about baby. She is in one of her moods. Drunk on cheap gin. Like always"

She just nodded. The events of the evening playing over and over in her mind. He looked at her and couldn't feel anything but disappointment. Didn't she see this was their big chance? Of course she didn't. Her life of privilege had just vanished. Suddenly she was no better off than him. He pitied her then and not for the first time. But he would make it all better. They would get married and raise a family and become successful on their own. They would prove everyone wrong. She would see. This was just a setback not the end. He would show her. They just sat out there for fifteen minutes lost in their own thoughts.

He was about to put the car into gear but stopped and remembered one more thing he wanted to take.

"I forgot something. Be right back," he told her and then went back into the house.

His mother was slumped back in the chair when he walked back into the room. The stocking gag soaked with vomit and the smell of bile and bleach. He held a hand mirror to her nose and saw no fog. A momentary panic hit him. He had killed her. He didn't mean to. It was just supposed to teach her a lesson. He stood staring at her limp body and the full gamut of emotions coursed through him. Disbelief to sorrow to a nice warm numbness. He untied her and laid her gently on her bed on her back and removed his grandmother's ring from her finger, the whole reason he had returned. He looked at her and felt that numb sensation fill him. He didn't care that she was dead. If anything he felt even more dedicated to the journey. How could he have truly moved on knowing she was still sitting her and cursing him? He couldn't he realized. It would have eaten at him. This was how it should end, with him closing the window and walking proudly out the door. Empowered by his own actions. Master of his own life and destiny.

He pocketed the ring and left the shack behind him. He made sure the windows and doors were shut as he left. Just to be on the safe side.

———

Ed tucked the gun into the back of his pants and made sure his shirt covered the tell tale bump as he stepped out of the car. A dog was barking from inside the big farmhouse. Two stories tall with peeling white paint and red trim, the house almost seemed to have a face watching his every move. When he shut the car door a light flickered on from the second story and he saw the curtains shift slightly from more than the light breeze that had set the weathervane squeaking as it proclaimed Northeast. He made a show of looking around, hoping to look slightly confused. Soon enough a light came on by the door and he did his best to seem small and unthreatening.

As the door opened his jaw dropped at the vision that well greeted him. She was petite with ice blue eyes that seemed to preternaturally glow in the night. Long brown hair with hints of red framed a heart shaped face. Full pouty lips and a smattering a freckles added a dimension to an already beautiful face.

"May I help you?" she asked him, a slight hint of fear and apprehension in her voice.

He tried to form words and found his tongue weighed down by the swell in his chest. Ed knew he had to respond but the words seemed to dissipate from his brain to his mouth.

"Sir? Are you alright?"

He shook his head and blushed a deep crimson that even the night couldn't fully hide. "I think I'm lost," he murmured stupidly.

Her worry faded as she saw the lost look on his face. He would have been proud of it working had it been planned in any way whatsoever. "Well where are you headed to?"

"I don't know anymore," Ed said and realized it was the truth. Everything fell apart back there. The end game of making it to Texas and raising a family was dead and blackened with Melody in the back of the Cadillac. He wouldn't, couldn't head back North. What was his goal now? Alone in the Ozarks of Missouri with a body count that kept growing the longer he was moving. And that was the other part of the issue - he didn't mind the killing. It had no effect on him at all. He wasn't sad or angry or excited by it.

He had just killed his fiancé and unborn child. Then two helpful strangers. And he hadn't even blinked. He always knew he wasn't like other people. That something seemed to be missing. It didn't seem important, whatever that part was that had withered on the vine inside of him. He felt things like love and anger. Like he could see the four points of a compass but the little directions escaped him. He realized it when his grandma died. He loved her. She was the only person that treated him with love and paid attention to him. But when she died he just carried on. He missed her but he missed lots of things. It just didn't matter that much.

But looking at her standing there, so demure and beautiful, he wanted to feel more. For a woman like this he wanted to be whole and real and sweep her off her feet. But he knew he could pull the pistol from his waistband and empty it into her full breasts and feel nothing. It frustrated him to no end. He could feel tears welling in the corners of his eyes.

And then his eyes grew as wide as half dollars as she stepped down the porch and gave him a hug and whispered, "It's okay. We'll figure it out. Don't worry."

He stiffened awkwardly and she pulled back, slightly embarrassed. "I'm sorry. You just suddenly looked so sad and helpless. My name is Michelle. Won't you come in? I can make us some coffee and try and figure out where you need to go."

"Ma'am, that would be delightful. Thank you. I'm Ed."

"Well come right in Ed, welcome to my little piece of paradise."

Ed smiled and followed her, shutting the door behind him. Michelle's house smelled like fresh baked bread and wildflowers. The worn wooden floors still maintained a luster and he could tell she prided herself on keeping her home tidy. Compared to the conditions he had grown up in this reminded him of the hospital he had spent plenty of nights in. A safe place where no one treated him like a pest. He could imagine growing old here. Sitting on the wraparound porch and watching the sunset.

Michelle hummed to herself as she prepared the coffee. Ed sat at the table and tried to think of a convincing story for why he was out here. The truth seemed like the wrong way to go. So much had happened since he and Melody had ran away from Wisconsin. It all began to crumble at the motel.

"So, tell me what is happening with you," she asked as she poured them each a cup. He stared at the lace fringe on the table cover as the coffee sent wisps of steam into the air. She sat silently spooning sugar and cream into hers, patiently waiting.

"I don't even know where to begin. Everything is just unraveling. We we're headed to Texas, maybe Mexico to start over. And then..." he trailed off.

"We?"

"My girlfriend, no, fiancé and I. Her parents didn't approve of us."

"And where is she now?"

"With her parents I guess."

He thought back to the motel.

Melody stayed in her despondent mood as he tried to get her excited about the road trip and new beginning. But she was beginning to see what she had lost when her parents told her to never return. He didn't understand, a happy family was as foreign to him as true joy. Just words he heard others use to describe something he would never have himself. They talked late into the night and finally she managed to cry herself to sleep. He sat watching her and knew as long as there was the kernel of hope she could go back home they would never be truly free. It would always be an anchor around their ankles dragging them deeper into the abyss.

He scribbled a note to her in case she woke and found him gone and left. He drove near her parents' house and parked a block away. He was careful to stay out of sight, not that the neighbors would recognize him. He had been Melody's dirty little white trash secret. They had always met somewhere else when they were together. But he knew the lay of the land, the long driveway and her parents' house nestled in a copse of tall trees. He stood in the huge backyard and stared pure venom at the place that was holding them back from their freedom. Anger flooded through him and he removed the small pocket knife from his front jeans pocket and cut down the clothesline. Then cut the rope into more manageable lengths.

He went in the back door which was usually unlocked. Melody didn't even know he knew this. She would have been shocked to know he knew the layout of the house intimately. That he had explored it extensively when no one was home. Her mother was allergic to animals so there was no dog to worry about. So he crept up the stairs to the main bedroom and stood in the doorway watching them sleep for a moment. Her father was laying with his arm wrapped around her mother. If he had to guess he would say they were talking and crying about the events of the evening and had passed out that way.

He continued down the hall to Melody's room. He loved how it smelled in here. Like sunshine and fresh laundry. Ed wondered if their child's room would smell like this. He hoped so. The only thing out of place in this dream world was the drawers of her dresser hanging open and empty. The closet door was ajar and he looked in and saw the hangers on the floor from where clothes were hurriedly pulled down and thrown into the suitcase her mother had thrust out the door with her words of no return. He opened it fully and removed the rod from the top, a solid inch piece of wood, three foot long, that was set on metal hooks at each end. He felt the heft of it against his open palm. This would do.

He walked tall back to the open bedroom door and watched them again. Lost in dreams and curled up together. So in love. But he knew the truth. He had seen the unbridled rage in his eyes as he beat on him earlier. The stiffness from it in his bruised muscles was still screaming. And he walked in and brought the wooden rod down on their sleeping forms, over and over again. The startled screams turning to exclamations of pain and then nothing but wet slapping sounds. He lost track of time as he pummeled them, only stopping when he realized the only sound was his hoarse meaningless anger. Their heads were like melons that fell out of a truck onto the highway in front of a bus.

He was covered in gore. The whole room was as it sprayed from the end of his makeshift cudgel. The mattress was soaked and he was surprised at the sheer amount of liquid in a human body. He opened the jewelry box on the bedside table and took what appeared to be the most valuable pieces. He found Melody's birth certificate and other assorted papers in a drawer and set then to the side.

He went to the bathroom and washed his face and arms off, not recognizing the face that looked back at him. When he woke up the morning before he was a different person. One with no direction and plan. Now he had murdered three people. He had become more. He was going to be a father. He had responsibilities. This was just a way of closing the last chapter so they could start a new one. He did it for them. For their unborn child. To spit in the eye of a world that had done nothing but hurt him. He wouldn't allow the world to do that to his family.

He was a man now. One firmly in control of his own destiny. He went back and found a white shirt and pair of pants, luckily her father and he were roughly the same size, and changed. He found another suitcase and filled it with Melody's old dolls and mementos from her room. He set the papers he had found in there as well and rooted around the house for anything else worth taking.

That was when he found the pistol and box of bullets in the top of her parents' closet tucked in the back corner. He smiled at the weight of it and looked down the sight. The Colt six shooter felt good in his hand. Reminded him of one of his mother's 'friends' that had treated him alright. The guy always had a gun in his car, for protection from black people he would say. He had taken Ed to learn to shoot one day out at the quarry. They set up bottles and tin cans and spent an afternoon blasting them away. Ed discovered he had a natural talent with firearms. Eventually the guy, Big Tom everyone called him, grew sick of his mother and her constant drinking and whoring and stopped visiting her. But he and Ed remained close and went out shooting every couple months. He encouraged Ed, a new concept for the boy then, and was impressed with his accuracy. Even considered getting him his own gun but with the volatile home life neither of them thought it was a good idea to have a weapon like that in the house.

Shaking himself from the reverie he went to the garage and grabbed the metal can of gas and liberally soaked everything, trailing it to the back door. Then he lit a cigarette and flicked it into the kitchen and made his way back to his car without a look back. He felt the heat on his back as he made his way through the bush with the suitcase and metal gas canister. He didn't know why he took it but it seemed like something to take on a road trip. Besides, he didn't think they would have much use for it.

When he returned to the motel Melody was in a panic. She woke up and read his note and worried he had gone and done something stupid. He just smiled and told her he had gone to try and talk sense into her parents. She lit up for a second but he sadly shook his head no and handed her the suitcase.

"Your parents wanted you to have this," he opened the suitcase and showed her the items that only really held value to her, "but they stand by what they said to us. They want us gone from their lives."

She clutched one of the dolls and cried as they loaded the car and left town as the sun rose.

She remained near catatonic as they drove through Illinois and got on Route 66. Every attempt to pull her out of the funk was met with silence or sobbing. Finally, when they stopped at a diner in Springfield, the capitol he told her, and drove past the big state building she perked up a little. As they sat eating cheeseburgers and thick cut fries, her favorite, she began to talk about the trip. He saw his opportunity to turn things around and dropped to one knee and proposed with his grandmother's ring. She stared at him for a long moment, the entire restaurant frozen on them, and burst out crying and said yes. The diners all broke into applause and they not only got their meal for free but two slices of the best cherry pie ala mode either had had.

Everything was looking up as they crossed the Mississippi River into St Louis. They even took a detour to see the big horses with the hairy hooves. She laughed at him and told him they were Clydesdales. He laughed at such a ridiculous name for an animal. It seemed they had turned the page to happiness again. They got a map of the state and after talking to some locals heard about a little lake in the Ozarks, Clearwater Lake and decided to go and see it. Maybe camp out for a couple days and fish and just relax in the outdoors before heading on.

They were in high spirits as they got off the main road and began to get deeper into the countryside. As the sun sank and they got farther and farther from cites and should have been close to their destination they discovered they were lost. Ed had been driving while Melody gave him directions based on the huge map on her lap. Somewhere along the line a left was taken instead of a right. It happens he assured her as she got upset with herself for the simple mistake. They just needed to pull over and try and figure out where it had occurred. He took the map and lit the lighter he had in his pocket to see with.

"Where did you get that lighter?" Melody asked pointing at the brass Zippo in his hand.

"I don't remember. Must have picked it up somewhere. Alright, I think we are around here..."

"Ed. That is my father's lighter," she whispered. "He would have never given that away. Not to you."

"What? No. This is my lighter. I took it from one of my mother's visitors."

"No it isn't. Don't lie to me Ed. I have seen that lighter since I was a baby. I know every scratch on it. Give it to me, I'll prove it."

"Melody, stop it."

"Give me the lighter Ed. Now!"

He shook his head and passed it to her, confused at the sudden outburst.

"There, his initials engraved on the bottom. This was a gift from his platoon leader in the army. Each member of the platoon got one when they got back to the States from Europe. Where did you get it?"

He knew exactly where he had gotten it. From the same bedside table that held the jewelry box in her parents' bedroom. "I must have accidentally pocketed it when I was talking to them before we left. I don't remember grabbing it."

"We have to go back. Now. We have to take it back to him immediately. He needs it. It is his good luck charm. He will be tearing apart the house searching for it," she told him. Her tone didn't leave room for questions.

"He will be fine. You're over reacting. He probably hasn't even noticed," Ed replied trying to calm her down.

"No." She began to open her car door and step out. Her foot hit the ground with a wet plop and he grabbed her arm to stop her. She shrugged him off and got out of the car. "Um, the car seems to be sinking into the ground. Ed, the tires are sinking into the ground and we have to go back home and take my father his lighter."

He got out as well and saw she was right. He hadn't paid any attention to the side of the road, just pulled off to get their bearings. He got back in and tried to pull away but the tires couldn't find any purchase in the muddy soil and sent a spray of muck into the air and sunk even deeper.

"Well this is just great. Lost in the middle of nowhere because you can't read a map and now we are stuck. When is the last time you saw a house?"

"My fault? I thought it was no big deal? A simple thing to fix? I didn't drive us off the road into a swamp in the middle of nowhere."

"I'm sorry. Melody, look I'm sorry. When we get to another town we can send the lighter to him through the post office. Okay? It will be fine. He'll have his good luck charm and we can continue. We just have to get unstuck."

She just looked at him with hurt all over her pretty face and crossed her arms.

"Okay baby? We just need to get out of this mess and everything will be fine again. Okay?" he asked her, a hint of pleading in his voice.

She shrugged and he wrapped his arms around her and looked into her eyes. "I am sorry. I got frustrated and shouldn't have taken it out on you. I love you Melody. It is going to be okay once we get unstuck."

Her expression melted and she returned the embrace and nodded yes into his chest. He squeezed her and then went to the trunk of the car in hopes of a magic solution to this mess. He dug around under the suitcase but couldn't find anything to use. That was when she saw the pistol he had stuffed by the spare tire and froze.

"That's my father's too." She reached in to grab it but Ed scooped it up first. "Why do you have his gun and lighter Ed? Why would you have both of those things? He kept the gun in the bedroom closet. You couldn't have accidentally..." and she looked at him, fear and revulsion contorting her face and began to back away from him.

"Look. I can explain this," he tried to calmly say. Her eyes were transfixed on the gun in his hand and he hurriedly tucked it into the back of his jeans. "This isn't what it looks like. There is a perfectly good explanation to all of this."

But she knew at that moment exactly what the reason was. Her father would never part with either of those two possessions. Especially not to Ed. He wouldn't give Ed anything but a beating. He hated him. Looked down on him and his whore mother. He had forbade she ever see Ed. Yet here was Ed with the lighter and gun. And he had come back to the motel in fresh clothes and smelled like gas. But in her sorrow she hadn't put the questions to word. Her life had fallen apart and he had come back revitalized and she had let him take charge. But now she knew why he was so excited to leave.

She quietly asked, "Did you hurt them?"

"No. Baby you have this all wrong."

"Don't lie to me. Did you hurt them?" The quiet steel in her voice had the hint of panic just brewing beneath the surface. Her entire body was trembling as she stared at him.

"Melody. Stop this. I went and tried to talk sense into them. They didn't want to hear it. I left. Must have accidentally grabbed the lighter on the way out. This Colt is the same one I used to shoot bottles at the quarry with Big Tom. I told you all about him. I must have left it in the trunk after we went shooting last week."

She just stared at him as if she had never seen him before and shook her head no. He reached out to her and she took a quick step back and slipped and fell onto her bottom. He made a move to help her up but she crawled backwards from him in terror.

"Don't touch me. Don't ever touch me again. What did you do to my parents? What did you do Ed?"

"Nothing. I swear. This is a misunderstanding baby. You have to believe me."

But they both knew it had gone beyond that. The cicadas sang loudly as they just looked at each other. Revulsion painted in her eyes as she saw the man her father had warned her about.

"He told me. He tried to tell me. He said you were trouble. Called you barely more than an animal. Said he knew guys like you in the army and that all that followed men like you was pain."

"It isn't like that."

"It is. He was right. And I think I knew it too. The poor son of the town whore. Never had two nickels to rub together..."

He was on her in a flash. Without thought. It happened so quick. He didn't even notice he had pulled out his knife. Didn't feel it enter her side. How it slid in between her ribs. It was one jumbled blur. And then he was carrying her to the side and gently sitting her against a tree as her life spilled out onto her white blouse.

He shook his head and took a sip of the coffee. He hated the stuff and as the bitter liquid ran down his throat he forced himself to look pleased with it.

"Oh Ed, I'm sorry. What happened?" Michelle asked him with genuine concern in her voice.

"She decided she would rather be with her parents than me." He was amazed as he felt something on his face and reached up to find it was a tear. "My mother had recently passed away and her parents didn't like me so we were going to make a fresh new life in the deep South. And then it all just fell apart."

"Oh you poor man. That is terrible. You have been through so much. How about you stay here for a spell and try and figure out your next step?" Her eyes seemed filled with concern.

He tried to respond but found he had a lump in his throat and couldn't speak. He just nodded and drank more of his coffee. It was disgustingly bitter. Even worse than he had remembered. He wished he had put sugar and cream into it to mask the flavor but didn't know if it would help. Michelle just watched him and lazily stirred the spoon in her own untouched cup.

And then he noticed he felt tired. More than tired. Exhausted. His head seemed to be swimming and his arms and legs began to feel like they were made out of lead. His eyelids began to drop as his vision darkened at the edges. What was wrong with him? Suddenly he didn't feel so good and needed to sleep. As his head began to fall towards the table he saw a smile on Michelle's beautiful face bloom.

"What's happ..." he murmured as his face slammed the table and then his body began to slump down out of the chair.

"Go to sleep Ed. You'll be with your mother soon..." was all he heard and then sweet blissful black took him away. He wanted to say his mother was dead but he felt like he had already told her he thought as consciousness left.

Michelle stood and pushed her chair back in and walked over to where he was unconscious on the floor. She patted him down and found the gun in his waistband and clucked with her tongue as she removed it. Then she reached into his pocket and removed the keys to his car. She went outside and opened the barn doors and pulled the car in next to three others that sat with a thick coating of dust on them. She worked efficiently and managed to get it into the far corner and place bales of hay around it to hide it. By the time she was finished the farm was waking up and she heard the rooster crowing. The coffee tin on the back floorboard had been a pleasant surprise with the amount of cash it held.

She carefully closed the big doors and brushed herself off and smiled. It was like her daddy always said to her, when God closes a door he sometimes opens a window. With the money and Ed to go into the larder for storage for the lean winter that would be on her soon she realized this time he had closed a window and she happily strolled through a door.

Coffee Trio

1) Coffee

"Get that fucking thing out of my face or I will force feed it to you."

So yeah, another morning and another knife in my face. The odds against this must be astronomical. This is the third time this week. I am getting awfully tired of the rigmarole.

And he was just another pathetic tool, too stupid to get a job, shaking in front of a coffee joint. I need to buy a coffee maker and just avoid this shit altogether.

"I said give me your credstick man," he drawled, thick hillbilly tone like mercury tinged molasses.

"And I said get that fucking thing out of my face."

His bloodshot eyes twitched and I knew what was coming next. Fucking psychemeth junkies. The knife came towards my face and I sidestepped to the left and slammed my elbow into his throat. A couple drops of coffee hit my wrist and it burned like hell so I planted my foot into his balls for good measure. He tried to let out an oof but the elbow shot made it sound more gravel filled. I picked up the knife and tossed it into the sewer as I made my way down the congested sidewalk.

Fucking tweakers.

The city was going to shit. Junkies on every corner making it hard to get a quick cup of coffee to kick start the motor neurons. And now my wrist hurt. I should have stayed in bed.

The next morning as I was exiting the coffee shop I saw the tweaker again. His now high pitched growl was punctuated with a plastic shiv. He saw me and made the right move and ran down the alley.

That made me feel slightly better about the prospects of my impending day.

It shouldn't have.

On my way home from the office, I say office but really mean barely standing building with water stained cubicles, I was accosted by a group of Knights of the Silence. Instead of knives they held pamphlets in my face. Embrace the Silence in boldface type with those funny lowercase Ts. A long day crunching numbers for the holovid business and a serious case of caffeine headache had left me irritable. And now these morons in their medieval armor pushing Silence and rattling a collection credstick did nothing to make it better.

"I am a devout Disembodied Head man gentlemen," I said as I tried to push my way through them. Some people just can't take a hint though.

"The Silence is all friend. He listens and judges from behind the gates of heaven. Come, listen to the gospel," the taller rust smelling Knight preached.

"Thank you, but my soul is going into the cryovats. Already paid my dues."

"The road to sin lies in not listening to the Silence. He watches and he judges."

"Tell him to stop being such a fucking creep then. Let me through rust bucket I got shit to do."

Luckily for me the tram let out and the teeming masses of easier marks came onto the street. Realizing I was not gonna give them a cred they moved on to better odds.

The tweaker was standing outside the coffee shop the next morning. He brought some friends with him today. Great. And I had bought a nice little danish and a double soy latte. Not the day to have a conflict.

He saw me and elbowed his friends to get their attention. Three tweakers who had clearly not showered this decade backed him up. I put my danish in my jacket pocket and could feel it get mushed as I did.

"Morning guys. Let me guess, the eunuch brought you along to give me a little payback? Just keep walking and no visits to the chop shop, deal?"

They did their best to look intimidating. I did my best to not miss as I unloaded the can of electromist into their faces. Soon it was me, my now ugly danish, and four twitching tweakers writhing in pain on the sidewalk. I kicked the one I knew in the balls again for good measure and gave him an extra spritz as I walked by.

Ruin my fucking danish. The nerve. More aptly, the nerve damage. Those guys did not look great.

I gotta get a coffee maker.

The sound of clicks behind me told me that the people in line were getting a kick out of seeing the junkies rolling around and were taking pics. Fucking tourists.

A whole week went by without incident. I think I set a record.

I finally bought a coffee maker off of the net. Supposed to be top of the line. It can even make espresso and lattes. I feel fancy.

Two problems though. One it doesn't have a feature that makes those danishes I like so much. Two I didn't read the fine print and this is one of those sentient units. I got a coffee maker with the personality replicant of some old time philosopher named Nietzsche. At first it was quaint.

At first.

But once it got started it never shut up. Scared the shit outta me the first time it spoke.

"Give me a soycaffe with two shots of espresso."

The hiss of heating water and smell of burnt soycaffe filled my little apartment.

"God is dead."

"What was that?" I asked, looking around.

"God is dead, man killed him." The coffee machine answered. What the fuck.

"He who fights monsters should take care lest he become a monster himself. Your coffee is ready. Life is meaningless."

The whole owning a coffee maker experiment lasted a week and a half. Soon good old Friedrich was in the alley. Probably depressing passing rats.

As a plus I got fresh danishes again.

And I saw the tweaker again my first day back. He was getting the courage to try and rob another shopper when he saw me. And I saw the front of his pants darken as his bladder let go. He turned and ran face first into the side of the building and hit the ground, blood pouring from his nose.

I love the City.

2) Coffee for Two

"Do you have any idea what you have done this time?"

She had a severe beauty. Like a freshly forged machete. Her green eyes like frozen emeralds glared at me. Her lips were pale from lack of blood as she spit the words at me.

"Most of the time, not really. Honestly. I just sort of go with things."

Her nostrils flared but in the cutest way possible. "You dumb bastard. Do you know how long I have been working on this?"

"Nope. Judging by the crease on your forehead, a while? Maybe?"

Her hand went to her forehead automatically to check for a crease. Shit. She is adorable. Wish she didn't hate me. That long red hair was an automatic turn on. If she wasn't pissed I think I would ask her out.

"I am beginning to hate you more every second. I have been watching them for three months now. And in five minutes you have ruined everything. Are you stupid?"

"Is that a trick question?"

She is right. I messed up big time. It wasn't my fault though.

———————

I used to run numbers for a holovid business. Easy gig in a not so easy area. A dangerous area to get coffee in I guess you could say. So I decided to try and move up the corporate ladder. Or step stool as it turned out. When I showed initiative and an urge to better myself the boss took that as a threat. Which turned into him threatening me. Which turned into me accidentally breaking his nose, hand and femur. Along with a couple fractures.

He spilled my coffee so technically he had it coming. I take my coffee very seriously. Except when it is brewed by a German nihilist. Not important.

So I found myself unjustly terminated from my position and in need of new employment.

Turns out assault with intent to cripple looks bad on a resume. So I followed my heart and applied as a security guard for a soycaffe warehouse. Reckless behavior and endangerment looks bad for an office but great for security apparently.

Score one for the good guy.

Nowadays most warehouses have pretty decent AI to handle the security. Expensive camera set up, infrared beams, the whole works.

This wasn't one of those warehouses. This was one of those shady warehouses that cut corners to increase profits and hired over qualified and less than rigid moral fiber guys to sleep in the office. And occasionally shoot rats with a company supplied pellet gun.

So I spent most of my nights working on my novel.

Gonna call it *Coffee World*.

Working title.

It is going to be huge. The main character is roughly based on me but trapped in a world far from here. A world without any men. They were all wiped out by a virus that is native to the atmosphere. He only survived because of his love for coffee which allows him to not only survive but thrive.

And all kinds of dirty sex as he tries to help repopulate the planet. So much sex. And coffee. Will practically print creds for me. Who doesn't love coffee and sex?

<hr />

So it is my third night and I may have somewhat hit the wall on coffee fueled sexcapades. Writing is harder than it seems, I figured any idiot could string together a few words. Punch it up with some violence and profanity. Easy.

Ugh.

You actually have to have an idea of where the story is going. Plot planning and shit. But I wasn't going to give up, this is a billion cred idea. Once I figure out little things like story structure and blah blah blah.

I was looking up book writing tips on the web when I heard a strange noise from the back of the warehouse. Thank the Silence. I grabbed my electromist can and job issued club. The club was a work of art. Perfectly weighted, ten k voltage, and just the cutest spike in the handle filled with scorpantula venom.

I honestly couldn't tell you if it was the erotica I was writing or the idea that I would get to use the club, but I was super aroused as I crept to the back of the warehouse.

And what did I see back there?

Serendipity my friends. The perfect synchronicity of the universe.

Digging through a crate filled with soycaffe beans of life was the familiar scarred face of my least favorite tweaker. And the similarly scarred faces of his crew of miscreants. We were old friends from back at the coffee shop. But what were they doing in the sacred caffe? I crept my way closer to them. They were pulling bundles of plastic wrapped something out.

This was going to be awesome.

I hit the button on my club and watched the voltage arc and stepped out of the shadows.

"Evening gentlemen. Afraid you are trespassing and I'm going to need you to lie on the floor before I pummel the ever living shit out of you."

They stopped what they were doing and turned towards me. And pulled guns out of their waistbands and opened fire. I threw myself to the floor as the erratic fire flew over me. They had really upgraded from the knives they used to use.

"Grab the stuff and go! He is just a rent a pig! He doesn't get paid enough to eat bullets. Right asshole?" that weaselly little prick yelled.

I hate to say it but he is absolutely right. I just crawled across the floor until I was sure I was hidden. The last thing the literary world needed was to lose my voice right as my masterpiece was being born.

"This is our business back here pig. We will be here once a week and if you wanna live you will stay in your office. Don't make us come and visit you."

That little piece of shit.

"Deal. I'm sorry to have bothered you."

"Yeah, that's what I thought chicken shit! You guys hear that pussy apologize?"

I listened to them laugh as I made my way back to my office. They didn't realize the mistake they had just made. The nerve of them. To use the sacred beans to smuggle contraband is an unthinkable crime against humanity.

I opened up my link to the special site. Next week was going to be a blast. Blaspheme the holy bean, time for righteous justice. Tweaker assholes one. Me zero.

For now.

It took me the rest of the week to set up the back of the ware-house. The Brain trust behind the smuggling had to dumb things down for the moron crew. Certain crates were marked with a big X in ultraviolet ink. It took me almost twenty minutes to figure it out. And once I did I popped open one of the crates. The plastic wrapped packages were psychemeth. Twenty pounds a piece, five per crate. By my math there was two thousand pounds of the stuff sitting back here.

Explains the lack of background check when they hired me. And the rigorous lack of security in the warehouse.

Days went by as I watched the cameras I had rigged up. Exactly seven days from the encounter the back door slid open and an unmarked thumper rolled into the warehouse.

I was practically giddy.

I let them open a couple crates. Watched their faces as they dug through only to come up empty handed. It took five crates for the wheels to turn in their meth riddled heads. And then they came for me.

I giggled. Actually giggled.

My plan was that they were half as stupid as I believed. As I followed them they proved to be more than twice as stupid. Instead of splitting up they came en masse down the center aisle.

I hit the center button on my new console.

As they walked with bravado towards my office they tripped the now active beam. The second they broke it three top of the line spinning betties popped up from the floor. I had modified them to disperse at roughly crotch level.

It was like a symphony. The beam broke. A gentle whizzing sound as the betties launched. And then the thwip thwip sound of three thousand neurotoxin tipped darts flying into the five idiot's crotches.

And then the screams of five tweakers as the toxin took all sensation from them starting at their testicles.

I let them writhe on the ground as the numb turned into what the site described as an intense burning. Best of all? One hundred percent legal home defense per City ordinance.

Then I called the police.

And laughed and laughed as I waited for the robots to come and clean up the mess.

After the police bots came and removed the screaming tweaker brigade and the psychemeth I had hidden I kicked back and began writing my magnum opus.

And that was when she stepped into the room. An Amazonian goddess with long red hair and eyes like green ice. She had been staking out the warehouse for three months, gathering intel on the psychemeth ring. Apparently my help set her back not just months but possibly years. The real brains behind the operation ran back into the shadows because of my little stunt.

I let her yell, content in my duty as keeper of the beans. My Silence ordained duty to law complete. And when she finally stopped calling me names I asked her out to dinner. Or maybe just coffee for two.

She refused. In the most imaginative way possible. I am still trying to work out the physics required to do what she suggested.

But in her refusal I got an even better thing. I had found the Queen of Coffee World.

The City isn't prepared for this work of art. Turns out writing is easy, it just takes the right idea and the perfect inspiration.

And plenty of soycaffe with extra espresso to fuel it.

This place is the greatest on Earth. I love the City.

3) Coffee World

...his heart raced from the caffeine that filled his bloodstream. He stood, rock hard, in front of his copper haired goddess. A sheen of sweat covered her entire, perfect body. Her voice was hoarse from the many, many orgasms that sent shudders through her frame. He didn't give her time to catch her breath though. He took her then and there. She moaned as his soycaffe soaked tongue entered her waiting mouth...

"And we are live with the author of the runaway success franchise, *Coffee World*. A former holovid analyst and security guard who used his love of coffee to fuel a sexual renaissance throughout the City."

"Glad to be here. Thanks for having me."

"Your bestselling book, now a major holovid has taken the City by storm. It is literally the talk of the town. And the question on everybody's mind, will there be more?"

"For sure. As long as there is coffee, there is fuel for the machine."

Fake laughter fills the studio. It lasts about thirty seconds too long.

But it feels good to be king.

I sort of zone out the rest of the interview. This is my third this morning. Writing the damn book was easy. Promoting it feels like a job. Don't get me wrong, I wanted the fame and creds that comes with it. Just didn't expect it to be such a pain in the ass.

Makes me wonder why people do it.

I guess they just need people to fawn over their every word. I did it for the coffee and sex. Thought it was pretty clear from the book itself. And with this schedule I have barely enough coffee and not nearly enough sex.

The price of fame.

Mental note to self, fire publicist and hire new one. Make sure next one understands I need down time between interviews.

After the warehouse security gig didn't pan out quite like I expected, and by that I mean once the drug smugglers were out of the picture the owners decided to put in real security and go legit, I found myself with a billion cred book idea and unemployed.

The sexy undercover drug agent filed a restraining order against me. No one was interested in hiring an accountant with a penchant for violence. I was stuck in my apartment drinking soycaffe with my thoughts.

Not the best place to be.

So I dove into my book idea. I threw the manual for writing out the window and realized whenever I hit a potential roadblock to just add sex and gore. It pretty much wrote itself from there. Danishes to feed the body, espresso to feed the mind, and smutty scenes to feed the masses.

And just wait for the creds to roll in.

My only issue was underestimating the public's desire for sex.

I had to install a thesaurus program to keep the words from being overused. Do you know how many different words there are that mean wet? Or hard? Not to mention moans, groans, rumbles and screams. At one point I just had the program auto fill wet slapping noises until I could go back and change it up.

And the kink factor! Sweet Silence these horny house wives wanted it dirtier and dirtier. My publisher got a test group together to read the manuscript and no matter how twisted the sex got they wanted more. Made me wonder if I made a mistake not getting married.

It got to the point where I couldn't tell if some of the acts were even conceivable. But the more improbable the better. Toys, torture, bondage, and oddly enough anything dealing with food made panties drop with a moist whoosh. Thank you thesaurus.

I began to fantasize about plain old missionary as a palate cleanser of sorts. I have done some weird shit in my life but, and feel free to call me old fashioned here, what a man, a woman, an artificial sex doll, a cloned sheep, three gallons of lube and a holovid of the apocalypse do in their own home is their business.

I say none of this. Just give polite answers to stupid questions. And mercifully it ends.

"Again, the book and holovid *Coffee World* are sweeping the City. Where can your fans find you next?"

"I am going to be doing some meet and greets at StarStrucks across the City the rest of the week. Looking forward to seeing my fans face to face and of course, drinking coffee with them."

"Her body writhed across the forest floor. Her screams sent birds from the trees around them. Fully engorged he yearned to penetrate her waiting, sopping womanhood. But he held back, the moment of desire calling, and teased her nipples with a slice of cantaloupe. The sweet melon, on her sweet round breasts, the perfect compliment to their sweaty forms. She licked the sugary juice from his fingers and he entered her. Gently at first, but driving need pushed him. He growled like a jungle cat and savaged her on the bed of leaves."

I hate reading out loud. But the gathered crowd ate up every word. Yelled for me to continue. It just felt wrong doing spoken word porno to these filthy minded bastards. No shower could clean me deep enough.

I should have used a pen name, a nom de guerre. Holed up in my penthouse suite and just counted the creds. But I let my hubris control me and went with my real name. And that meant the public knew me.

It took a week before I started receiving gifts. At first innocent love letters. Then progressively weirder things. Used panties. Paintings of me as the main character, Chuck Java, with what I can only guess were the likeness of the artist and I having sex. One painted in blood. Menstrual blood. That one hangs in the bedroom.

Don't judge.

Marriage offers, death threats, death threats if I didn't accept the marriage offers, a whole laundry list of obsessive behavior. It is a real kick to the ego. In the best possible way.

The horny masses lined up to say hello. Some brought stuff for me to sign. I didn't mind signing the occasional breast or poster. That was fine. One lady had me sign her arm and she immediately went to have it tattooed. Okay. Sure. But the sheer number of dildos that these hands touched and signed, and not all sanitized I might add, was shocking.

Disturbing and downright disgusting.

As the line dwindled it was like an open air fish market on my hands. If I didn't think I would need a new phone after touching I would look up where I could get a full body alcohol dip to kill the certain thousands of sexually transmitted diseases I might have contracted.

Did I rub my eyes? I hope to the fucking Silence I did not.

Eww.

I was digging in my bag for an EpiPen just in case I went into toxic shock when I heard a voice that sounded like gravel mixed with a prepubescent boy.

"I love your work. So much. It speaks to me. Got me through a bad time in jail."

I looked up and nearly flipped the table. The fucking tweaker was staring at the ground holding out a pocket pussy for me to sign. What are the odds that this sad sack of shit would stumble into my life again?

"Hey Tweak. Remember me?" I said as I looked horrified at the poor sexual implement in his twitchy hand.

His face went pale and he dropped his toy. It made a satisfying squelching sound as it hit the floor. His hands went to his crotch instinctively.

"You? You? Those needles made my dick numb for six months! You are a psychopath! What the fuck man. What the fuck!"

Security came forward, hands on their electromist cans. I waved them off and stepped from behind the table. I thought my head would split in half from the smile on my face.

"The scars have nearly faded Tweak! You look great!"

I turned him to the crowd and put my arm around his shoulders. I could feel him sobbing. The crowd grew silent at this unexpected moment.

"Ladies and gentlemen, we have a real treat here. I would like to introduce you to Tweak, the inspiration behind the man Chuck Java left Earth to get away from! This is the sack of shit that tried to rob, shoot and rough me up so long ago."

The crowd ooohed and ahhhed at this. I looked at Tweak and said, "Take a bow kid." And then slapped him in the balls. Applause rang out as he doubled over, drowning out his cries.

Some days it really pays to be a writer.

I screamed at the top of my lungs to my adoring fans, "I fucking love this City!"

"With one final thrust, Chuck exploded inside of her. The potent force of a triple shot of espresso and their love erupting in a glorious climax. They lay together exhausted as the Amazons cheered. The sounds of chains rattling muffled by the celebration. The remains

of the fruit basket discarded around the throne room. Their bodies entwined, both knew he had fulfilled his duty and planted his seed deep within her. In the morning he would begin again, the repopulation of an entire planet a job he took on with relish. For he was Chuck Java, King of the Amazons on Planet Vagene. And this was where he belonged.

CUSTOMER SERVICE

8:53 am.

"Customer Service, this is Brandon. How may I help you today?"

"Hi Brandon, my name is Edgar. I recently purchased your 5800 series Pocket Pussy and am having some difficulties with the product at the moment."

"What seems to be the problem?"

"It is clamped onto my penis and nothing I have tried will get it off."

"Did you remove the batteries?"

"Yes. My balls are turning blue; I've had this thing stuck on me for over three hours now. I really need to get it off. I'm already late for work and I can't just say I have a fuck toy latched onto my cock."

"Have you tried to manually force the labia apart? If you grasp it firmly and apply pressure at the clitoral area and bottom it should automatically open."

"I've tried all of the recommended ways of getting the fucking thing off; none of them are fucking working! Do you think I would have called and told someone about this if I hadn't tried every other fucking method?"

"Please relax sir; I understand that you are in an uncomfortable situation. Please hold for a moment while I speak with my supervisor about this."

"Wait! I don't have time for this shit!"

"Thanks for calling Fukco; your call is important to us. Please hold for our next available representative. Remember at Fukco, you are like family."

"This is just fucking great! Stupid fucking Pocket Pussy, never should have bought it. Stupid fucking girlfriend and her goddamned space!"

*"...I don't want anybody else, when I think about you I touch myself. Ohhh, I don't want anybody else, oh no, oh no, oh no...*Customer Service, this is Frederick. How may I help you?"

"I'm on hold with Brandon. He went to speak with the supervisor and should be back any minute."

"Brandon just got off of his shift; I passed him in the hallway as I was coming on. How may I assist you?"

"I have a goddamned Pocket Pussy stuck on my cock and I need the Jaws of fucking Life to pry it off! That's how you can fucking help me! Get this fucking thing off of me!"

"Please calm down sir. Did you say you have a Pocket Pussy stuck on your penis? Is it the model 5800 or 6000?"

"It's the 5800 series cocksucker! I can hear you laughing! What the fuck kind of place do you work for!? I want to speak to your fucking manager!"

"I can make any decision that my manager can sir, and I would appreciate it if you used a different tone with me. I understand you are under some stress at the moment but that doesn't give you the right to yell and use profanity at me."

"Are you fucking serious? One dumb fuck puts me on hold and goes home and then you come and can barely snicker under your breath and I need to calm down? Just tell me how to get this fucking thing off of my cock and we'll call it even!"

"Sir, I will ask you one more time to please refrain from yelling at me. I am trying to help you in this unfortunate situation. Have you tried to remove the batteries yet? If not, I would recommend doing so now."

"I removed the batteries and it remained in a Vise-Grip on my dick. You need to understand that my fucking balls are blue and I am late for work. Forgive me for seeming testy but how do I get this Chinese finger trap off of my dick?"

"Testy? That was truly an appropriate term for this, now wasn't it?"

"Are you trying to make me start fucking screaming? My fucking dick is numb! Do you understand what I am fucking saying here? *MY FUCKING DICK IS NUMB!*"

"I'm sorry sir, but if this is how you are going to act then I can offer no help to you. Thank you for calling Fukco, good day."

"Don't you dare hang up that fucking phone! You hung up that fucking phone!"

9:06am.

"Customer Service, this is Alicia. How may I help you today?"

"Hello Alicia, my name is Edgar and I was just on the line with Frederick. Is there any chance I could talk with your manager? See, I have a rather large problem and need to get it resolved as fast as possible."

"Sir, I can do anything that my supervisor can to help alleviate your problem. How may I be of service?'

"Alicia, I understand you are willing to help but is there any chance I can speak with a male operator?"

"Are you saying I can't help you because I am female sir? I will have you know I am just as qualified as any of the men we have working in this company. In fact, I have a good deal of seniority over most of my male co-workers. Now how may I help you?"

"I have a 5800 series Pocket Pussy clamped on my dick in a grip of death. My balls are turning purple and my shaft has gone numb. The batteries are out of the fucking thing and I have pushed on the clit and pulled at the lips with everything I have."

"Please hold while I get my supervisor to handle this call."

"Here at Fukco, we offer a large variety of novelty items for bachelor and bachelorette parties including our brand new double ended muscle massager- The VibroMax Duo 3000! It has been voted top honors by the Adult Film Association. Also try our newest 6200 VibroTwat! There is no quicker way to satisfy an urge than with this self lubricating pleasure toy. A study of over 100 truck drivers says they would rather have sex with their wives than with any other item on the market! (this line doesn't make sense) At Fukco we are only thinking of you, our most valued asset."

9:11 am.

"...God is watching us, God is watching us, God is watching us...from a distance... This is Thourogood, How may I be of assistance today?"

"I'm sure Alicia has filled you in on my little situation. How do I get this fucking thing off of my dick?"

"Excuse me?"

"The Pocket Pussy that is dangling off of my cock! HOW DO I GET IT OFF OF THERE?"

"Sir, did you just say that there is something dangling off of your penis? I would recommend calling an ambulance as quickly as possible."

"Are you fucking with me? Are you seriously fucking with me? I have had this thing on my dick for what feels like a lifetime now. Everything has gone numb, my balls are purple and starting to swell, and I am in no fucking mood for a comedian. How do I remove this fucking thing from my penis?"

"Sir I just had this call transfer over to me, I think your call may have been transferred over here on accident. I am a rep for the Christian Care Center and help line. I can transfer you back to the other side of the building where the Fukco staff is located. They recently upgraded our phone systems and no one is quite sure on how to work them yet. Fukco and the Christian Care Center are sister companies under the True Life umbrella of companies and we share space in the same building. I can send your call back over there immediately."

"Is this some kind of sick fucking joke you play on people? Passing me around so everyone can hear my story and laugh at me and then making up this bullshit story to keep me on the fucking line? You can go fuck yourself Thourogood. Put your goddamned manager on the fucking line right now asshole!"

"Please hold sir, God bless you and I hope you have a wonderful day."

"At the Christian Care Center, we believe that God can help us through any of life's setbacks. With the power of faith and love; there is nothing that cannot be accomplished. We were recently voted the top Christian care group in the main 48 states. Soon we will expand to provide the Lord's teachings around the world with the help of loyal supporters like yourself."

9:17 am.

"This is Donnell, how may I help you today?"

"Well Donnell, this is Edgar. As I told the last bunch of dickheads my fucking penis is stuck in your goddamned Pocket Pussy."

"Is it the 5800 or the..."

"It is the fucking 5800 model. So help me God if another one of you pricks asks that question again or transfers me to another fucking retard I will come down there and burn the fucking building down! I want my dick out of this little deathtrap and I want it done now!"

"Sir, I understand your obvious discomfort, and we here at Fukco have nothing but the utmost respect for someone in your, shall I say, difficult circumstance. But if you cannot refrain yourself from using both profanity and the threat of violence I cannot do anything but disconnect this call. Now please, once again, repeat what the exact problem you are having is."

"You listen dingle berry shit for brains cocksucker! Your shitty little sex toy has decided to latch on to my cock like a baby calf to the mother fucking udder! You want me to refrain from profanity as my balls swell to the size of grapefruits and my dick grows cold from lack of circulation? I hope someone beats you to death with an entire crate of Pocket Pussies! Get me your fucking manager this fucking instant!"

CLICK

10:38 AM.

"911, what is the emergency?"

"He came in here screaming about his penis! He has all these gas cans and he is pouring gas on everything!"

"Sir, I need you to calm down. Can you describe the person for me?"

"Average height I guess, brown hair, and he has a 5800 series Pocket Pussy hanging out of the zipper of his pants! He keeps screaming he has rubbed the clit until it fell off! It is stuck!"

"I will send a unit out immediately sir. Get yourself and anyone else you can out of the building until help arrives."

"Please just hurry! Oh God he has a gun and he's shooting! Oh shit, Donnell is down. Please hurry! He is insane!"

"Just get yourself to safety sir, help is on the way. I wonder if he removed the batteries?"

"I asked him that and he snarled and tried to douse me with gas too."

INTERVIEW

"Hello, Mark? Great to see you, welcome. I'm Kyle, your first meeting of the day. Did you find the building okay?"

"I did, my phone did all the work honestly. I just punch in the address and do what the lady says."

"I understand that, been married for ten years. My life is based around doing what the lady says."

"Right. Sounds like you know how to play the game."

"You have no idea, please take a seat. Give me a second to pull up your résumé here. So how did you hear about us?"

"I drive past here all the time. The other day I decided to stop in and fill out an application."

"Great. No one recommended the job, no website?"

"Nope, like I said I just took a chance."

"Nothing on the news? No articles?"

"No sir. Is there something I should know?"

"Not at all my friend, just questions on the form here. So have you ever done customer support before?"

"Did a little sales cold calls for a while right out of high school. Insurance and credit cards. Been in retail the last couple years and waited tables a bit."

"Well this is different, we are an inbound call center. You will take an average of ten calls a shift. We have an intensive training program and tools for troubleshooting."

"I am pretty good with my hands and a quick study, it shouldn't be too hard."

"Great attitude, we like that kind of outlook here at Plastivag Inc. A little about us, we have been around since 1887, founded by Dr Hugh Döng. Dr Döng had been researching medical procedures involving penile enhancement and virility. He pioneered the act if milking the prostate."

"Did you say milking the prostate?"

"Otherwise known as the male g-spot, yes. Before his studies it was thought the penis was the only male erogenous zone. Very cutting edge at the time. His breakthroughs reinvigorated the world of sexual exploration."

"Umm. What exactly do you do here?"

"Did you not read the information our HR department sent to you? This was all covered in the interviewee package."

"I must have missed that one."

"Is this going to be a problem, Mark?"

"No sir, just took me by surprise is all. Please continue."

"Excellent. So we are over a hundred years old as a company. We have gone through a few corporate restructures lately, shifted our focus to better reflect customer care and our dedication to supplying the best product for the most important people on the planet. Our customers."

"Cool."

"Believe me Mark, it is. We are the cutting edge of sexual devices. Last year we released our first robotic companion and our stock prices tripled. This year we plan to release 2.0 and estimates put our profits on par to eclipse the last five years. It is an exciting time to be a member of Plastivag."

"What is your role here?"

"I am in charge of the vibrators and anal plugs. Been with them for the last three years. Before that I was in advertising.

But when I first came on I was customer support. We believe in raising from within."

"That sounds great. I want my next job to be my last job."

"Why would you say that? What does that mean?"

"That I am tired of starting over. Sorry, did I say something wrong?"

"My apologies Mark. Too much coffee this morning. One of the perks of the job is gourmet coffee. Between that and exciting innovations in how people view sex, it makes things..."

"Stimulating?"

"Exactly! We have this new product about to be unveiled that is going to change butt plugs and the way people view them. We pioneered the butt plug tails ten years ago when we introduced the cat, rabbit and fox plugs. This new model will be a revolution. Without giving away too much, think plumage."

"Like a peacock?"

"How in the hell? Yes, exactly like that. Imagine being able to not only walk around fully engorged but with one of fifteen designs letting the world know exactly what you have going on back there!"

"Um."

"Customers have been dreaming of this for the last ten years. And that is the tip of the iceberg. Imagine a fully robotic tail, with the ability to eat with or grab your keys off of the table. Like a third arm that fits directly into the anal cavity."

"Never considered that before."

"Prepare to be blown away then. The future is wide open, and we hope to make everyone else as well."

"You are definitely enthusiastic."

"You will find that is the Plastivag way. Well it seems we are all set here. Let me go get Chris and Denzil, they are the support leads and will take over from here. Thank you very much and it was a pleasure talking with you."

"Thank you Kyle, hopefully we will be seeing more of each other soon."

"Hopefully. Good luck. This multiple interview process can be a beat down, but it is the Plastivag way. I will turn up the music for you while you wait."

"Thanks."

...butts and I can not lie You other brothers can't deny That when a girl walks in with an itty bitty waist And a round thing in your face You get sprung, want to pull up tough 'Cause you notice that butt was stuffed Deep in the jeans she's wearing I'm hooked and I can't stop staring Oh baby, I want to get wit'cha And take your picture My homeboys tried to war...

"Mark? Hi, I'm Chris and this is..."

"...Denzil. Nice to meet you. First time going through a gauntlet style interview?"

"Nice to meet you both. Yes it is. It is daunting."

"We all said the same thing when we went through it. Trust us, make it through this..."

"...and it is all smooth sailing. Plastivag is a great company. We like to refer to it as..."

"...the Google of fuck toys. After the, um, fire we renovated most of the building. Gutted out the old and rebuilt at the cutting..."

"...edge of technology. And that all starts in the basement..."

"...with customer support. And that is us, and maybe you. Questions?"

"There was a fire? How long ago was that?"

"You don't know? Seriously? It must have been..."

"...six years ago. It made the news."

"I don't really watch the news. Or surf the internet. Never been my thing. I read a lot and play video games."

"No shit. What are you playing? Lin and I just got..."

"... the new Call of Duty. Been trouncing fools online. You play?"

"Not really, maybe campaign mode. I like rogue types and jrpgs mostly. How long have you guys worked here?"

"Funny story there, we got hired the same day. It was..."

"...six years ago. They had a bunch of..."

"...unexpected openings and we jumped at the chance."

"And look at us now. I am on track to get promoted over to the coding side of the building..."

"...and I am in line for advertising. Been a dream of mine since I can remember. Ever see the old ads..."

"...for the original Iron Cock? That supplement changed the game. Before Viagra and Cialis. The competition is stiff..."

"...all you can do is get stiffer! Fukco, the name that means pleasure..."

"...so pleasure yourself today!"

"Did you guys know each other before this?"

"Everyone always asks us that. We..."

"...met that day. Love at..."

"...first sight."

"Right. So how is the job itself?"

"Honestly, it is easy as hell. The phones barely ring and..."

"...all of our products are super customer friendly. It is easy money."

"And the people that call in? I mean, it is a strange group that calls a sex toy helpline, right?"

"Are you talking about..."

"...six years ago?"

"The fire? No. I am just trying to get my head wrapped around the job itself."

"Sorry man. Everyone has been on edge and the hiring..."

"...process is always hard on everyone involved."

"Too much coffee. I get it."

"Great. Honestly this is a great job..."

"...with great people. You will love it here. Oh snap, look at the time..."

"...we will go get Alexa. She is our supervisor. Watch out for that one..."

"...she can be a real monster bro. Just kidding. Have a great rest of your day."

"You too. Thanks a lot guys. Hope to see you again."

...take me baby, kiss me all over, play with my love, bring out what's been in me for far too long, Baby you know that's all I been dreaming of...

"Mark? Hi, I'm Alexa. I am in charge of customer service here at Plastivag. How are you today?"

"Fine. Nice to meet you."

"So you just had Tweedle Dum..."

"...and Tweedle Dee. Yes. They were certainly, um, unique."

"One day we all assume they will run off together and get married. It is a very strange, symbiotic relationship."

"Right."

"So did they fill you in on the job? Backstory, Role?"

"Not so much. Basics; the people are great here. The job is fun. The fire and renovation..."

"They mentioned the fire? What else did those morons bring up?"

"That it is a state of the art building. Nothing else."

"Goddamn them. They were told specifically not to me ntion... sorry. Yes the job is great. We manufacture the best sex toys and robotic sex partners on the planet. Like the real thing only better. And you don't have to fake a relationship to get laid with our products."

"Ha-ha."

"I am dead serious. I was engaged before I started here. The first time I took home the Donkey Puncher 3000 I realized what true love is. Clitoral stimulator, fourteen phase pulsating heads on the shaft, g-spot hook, anal attachment. Excuse me, I get wet just thinking about it. Two days later I broke off the engagement. That was three years ago. Five advancements later and now I run customer support."

"Um, wow."

"Damn right wow. As a matter of fact right now I have Twat Blaster 2.0, an integrated panty device on. Remote control operated by bluetooth. It uses an app downloaded to smartphones to change profiles and operating speeds."

"Well you are definitely sold on the products. What type of calls are typical on these devices?"

"Normal stuff you would expect. Password reset, how to change batteries, occasionally physical resets in some of our older models."

"Physical reset?"

"Some of the older models of pocket pussy had issues with locking on during self stimulation. The clit is the release button, along with the added benefit of teaching men where the clit was located. Dr Döng was very big in recreating the vagina down to the most intimate details. He actually patented the first self lubricating pocket pussy with scented lubes. He was an aficionado on the different smells and proudly recreated his top ten favorites. Rumor is he was working on flavors as well. I heard he had an agreement with Starkist on branding them."

"That is, wow. Um, Starkist Tuna?"

"Mhmm. The one and only. Every couple years a hot shot engineer tries to recreate that lightning in a bottle. Last year we introduced Yoga Pants - Hot Yoga limited edition. As you can imagine it was an instant sell out."

"I can only imagine."

"Dr Döng was ahead of his time. He was the one who bought out, non-typical companies and brought them under our original Fukco brand of products. We are home to one of the largest Christian outreach call centers as well."

"Seriously?"

"Being in touch with one's sexuality does not preclude religion. You can be in touch with yourself and God. In fact if you join us you will share floor space with their call center."

"Has anyone ever gotten the wrong call center when calling in?"

"Why do you ask? That is a very oddly specific question Mark."

"Curiosity more than anything."

"Are we perfect? No. Mistakes happen. But we work tirelessly to prevent it. I'm sorry, can I have a moment? My boss just texted me and I need to see what he needs."

"Sure. No problem."

"Here, I was going to have you watch this video of Dr Döng's grandson, Dr Pierre Eckert, explaining what our business means to him."

"Sounds interesting."

"Be right back. Enjoy."

Hello, my name is Dr Pierre Eckert and I am the grandson of Dr Döng the founder of Fukco. We would like to welcome you to the home of sexual freedom.

150 years ago, my grandfather sought to cure the blight of erectile dysfunction and help men and women reach the wonderful world of orgasm. He left London and came to the states, first to Chicago and then settling here in Dallas in the early 30s. And since then it has been our mission to keep the planet cumming. From the Bionic Fist to the AssMaster 68 we have not only done that but we have refined the sexual experience of over 100 million satisfied customers.

I myself have used every iteration of the RoboTwat, the Prostate Milker, and the Ball Fondler 1850. In fact, I have our newest Male Enhancer Butt Plug in right now. And it is a delight.

"Jesus Christ."

Trust me, I wouldn't have you put it inside if I didn't try it out first, that is the Dr P Eckert promise, and a Plastivag guarantee. Stop by the front desk on your way out and take a complimentary RoboTwat 2000 as our way of saying thank you for your time.

"Pretty impressive, right?"

"Oh damn, you scared me."

"Sorry. There is a RoboTwat 4000 waiting for you though. A little thank you for running the gauntlet as we like to call it. The 2000 has been discontinued as of five years ago. They go for big money on EBay."

"You don't have to do that. I have a fiancé."

"Maybe you will change your mind on that after trying it out."

"Hmm."

"I doubted it as well. It is okay, healthy doubt is a sign of intelligence. So do you have any questions for me?"

"I get the basic gist of the job. I am sure if I get it I will have a million questions but for now I am set."

"Awesome. Well it was a pleasure talking with you Mark."

"I feel the same. Thank you."

"Let me go and get Lin for you. He is our escalation engineer and works hand in hand with customer support."

...clock on the swatch watch, no time to chill, got a date, can't be late Hey this girl is gonna do me, move to the jacuzzi, ooh that booty, smack it up, flip it, rub it down, oh no

do me baby, (yeah), do me baby, (I like it just like that), do me baby, (oh yeah), do me baby, (oh move just a little bit closer)

you can do me in the morning, you can do me in the night, you can do me when you wanna do me...

"Oh damn! This is my jam! Hey there, my name is Lin, escalation engineer and coolest guy you will meet today."

"Mark, nice to meet you."

"Who have you met with so far?"

"Kyle started it off."

"Mr. Butt Plug himself, didn't shake his hand did you?"

"Well..."

"I'm kidding man. He is a good guy. There is a stick up his ass joke somewhere here though.."

"Ha. Right."

"Chris and Denzil were next."

"Those are my boys! We play Call of Duty all the time. Did they do the whole finish each other's sentences thing the whole time?"

"Yes."

"They just need to fuck and get it over with. Seriously. And then you had Alexa. Did she tell you about her panties? Of course she did. She talks about them all the time. One time we figured out her password and when she was in a meeting we turned it all the way up. Dude. She was trying to stop it and crossing her legs like a cricket. It was hilarious."

"Sounds like harassment."

"What?"

"Sounds hilarious, like you said."

"Oh, for sure man. You never know what can happen here."

"Like the fire?"

"Definitely. I was there that day. Crazy shit man. No one expected that to go down like it did."

"What happened? Everyone gets all kinds of twisted when it gets brought up."

"You don't know? Oh man, we are not supposed to talk about that night. Like at all. Google that shit man. I can't believe you don't know about it."

"But..."

"Sorry dude. No can do. Anyway. What makes you want to work in the exciting field of fuck toys?"

"I didn't know that was what happens here."

"Oh shit. Bet that was a surprise."

"Like you would not believe."

"It is no big deal man. Honestly you barely have to do anything here. And if you do the rest of the team has your back. Well, almost everyone. Gotta watch out for the lead, dude will sell you down river to make himself look good in a second."

"Really?"

"Oh yeah. As fake as they come. We call him the Chameleon."

"Why?"

"He has no personality of his own. Dude tries to be exactly like whoever he is around. No life, no real friends, just this job and whoever he can blow to make himself look better. Put it this way, his only real friend is his mother. Calls her everyday on his way home to tell her how great he is."

"His mom is his only friend?"

"I know a guy who went to school with him and said it has always been that way."

"His mom?"

"Yup. Wait until you see him. He is like six foot four, easily pushing 450 pounds. Body acne from not being able to wash that girth correctly. Smells like salty shit all the time."

"That doesn't sound healthy."

"He ignored me outside of a Chipotle once. I hold grudges. We are work cool through."

"Wow, sounds like it. I don't want to work in a drama filled cesspool. I have been a server before and remember how the back worked."

"No, this place is the best. I have been here ten years. Had other offers but this is the place for me. Anyway, about me, so I just broke up with my girl of seven years and have been out playing the field. Lotta strange out there my man. Been tearing it up. Me and my boys hit up the clubs."

"Cool. Why don't you just use some of the products from here?"

"Like Alexa? Naw. I like real pussy that plastic and rubber just doesn't do it for me. I mean, I have some stuff at home but you know."

"I honestly do not."

"Damn. I forgot that already. You'll see, everyone gets curious and tries it out. They give you a 4000 just for coming in. Ask them to throw in some of that fresh out of the shower gel."

"What about the job, I really need this."

"Dude, if you made it this far it is basically yours. One more interview and then we all gather and do a round table and discuss if you should get the job. But between you and me, your lack of knowledge about this place is more in your favor. Other applicants come in and think they know all about Plastivag and what happened six years ago. That is like the worst thing they could say."

"Okay. Shit. Makes me just as nervous."

"Don't sweat it. Now the next guy you have to talk to is a total badass. In his own head. Just nod and smile and he will give you the okay. With him and me and Chris and Denzil you got four outta six for sure. Kyle doesn't care and Alexa needs bodies. Total cakewalk."

"Thanks man, that makes me feel way better."

"Sure homie. Shit, let me go get him. You and Alexa went a bit over and all I planned on was talking shit about these fools and that was a success. It is kind of what I do. We work on rubber fists and butt plugs, technical is not really needed here. But they have college reimbursement. I am like five years from my bachelor's."

"Nice. Been working on it a long time?"

"Yeah man, the last four years. I do one class a semester. Ain't got time for more between this and all the strange. Hey if you get bored add me on Xbox. FrankenLin69. Later."

"I will."

There was a time when you let me know what's really going on down below, but now you never show that to me, do you? But remember when I moved in you and the holy dove was moving too and every breath was Hallelujah

Hallelujah, hallelujah, hallelujah, hallelujah

Maybe there's a God above, all I've ever learned of love, was how to shoot...

"Mark, nice to meet you. Richard, I am the national development and testing manager for Plastivag. Welcome to our little building where dreams come true."

"Nice to meet you sir."

"So you have nearly made it through the gauntlet. What a crazy day, right?"

"It is unique."

"Unique? I like it! I am going to use that. That describes this entire building. So you and Lin seemed to bond, he has been here a long time. Only Grady, the customer support lead has been here as long. You would have met with him typically but he is just far too busy today. If you come on you need to keep close with him."

"Lin?"

"No, Grady. If we could have five of him we would be unstoppable!"

"Great."

"So what kind of experience do you have with our products?"

"Well, see. None. I was not aware of what happened here. Just stopped in on a whim to fill out an application."

"What do you mean what happened here?"

"That I did not know what type of business this was."

"Oh. Okay."

"It isn't like there is a sign with a vibrator on it outside."

"True. Hard to advertise it and not risk people having an issue about it. Everyone has sex but the majority consider it dirty and not to be talked about. Funny part is the same people that would protest are our most loyal customers."

"I can see that."

"Yes, the inherent contradiction was not lost on Dr Döng, he embraced it. You know about the largest Christian care organization being under the same umbrella as Plastivag, right? He knew that by bringing the two together he could help bridge the gap."

"Smart."

"He was next level. When he was seventeen, or so the story goes, he was... can you give me a moment, I need to take this."

"Of course."

"Thank you. This is Richard. Code blue! Lock it down, immediately, I will be right there. Look Mark, we have a situation on our hands and I am going to need you to stay here until it is over."

"Um, what kind of situation? Like six years ago?"

"We do not mention that period. But yes, code blue signifies a breach in our building."

"Oh fuck me. Fukco. It has been scratching the back of my brain all day. The dude with the pocket pussy clamped on his dick that burned down the building and killed fifteen people. I do remember. I never knew it was this place."

"That is correct. And we have a situation again."

"How often does this sort of thing happen with you fucking people?"

"Three, maybe four times a year. Last time the guy's robotic partner malfunctioned and ripped his penis off."

"Fuck me. And you just don't mention this during the span of five interviews? What the fuck man?"

"It makes the hiring process difficult."

"You are a sick piece of shit."

"Maybe, but the Plastivag way is to keep moving forward always. Do you know how many vagrants were used by Dr Döng to further his research? He studied them, dissected and modified them."

"Has no one ever put him and Jack the Ripper or H.H. Holmes together?"

"Excuse me?"

"Same time frame, same weirdly sexual bend. The dude that created the Fist Pumper may have been one of the most famous serial killers of all time."

I want to sex you up

"I need to answer this. This is Richard. Okay. Do we have eyes on him? Well why the fuck not? If I understand correctly he has the Two Phase Pocket Pussy Anal Pounder stuck on his fucking body. Look for someone with five pounds of plastic and rubber hanging off his goddamned genitals and shoot to fucking kill!"

"Look, I am just going to leave. You guys have this under control and I am not sure this is exactly the job for me. I appreciate the time you have spent with me."

"We are under lockdown Mark. The doors are sealed until the event has been taken care of. Until they subdue the intruder we are stuck together in this room."

"Fucking awesome."

"I am not happy about this either. I survived this six years ago and no goddamned pervert is going to get me this time either."

"Everyone brings up six years ago but no one ever wants to talk about it. What the fuck did you guys do?"

"This was before we had scripts and made standard work our standard practice. It was not our fault at all, if they were not sealed I could show court documents proving it. A gentleman called in with a personal sex enhancer locked onto his penis. He called in, highly agitated and using improper language."

"Understandably. His dick was locked in a machine."

"Etiquette is the only thing that separates us from the animals Mark. We follow protocol here at Plastivag. An angry customer is beyond words. He was disconnected."

"You hung up on him?"

"He continued calling in. There were some, unforeseen phone line issues. We had just installed a new system and he was bounced around a bit. We receive these calls quite often. This was nothing new."

"But it became something new. You repeatedly hung up or transferred a dude with his cock stuck in a pocket pussy."

"Again, we did nothing wrong. Followed typical protocol for instances like this. The emergency release on his, ahem, unit was faulty. Instead of releasing the device it was incrementally tightening it. A one in a million malfunction we were not prepared to handle."

"So it was a Vise-Grip on his junk, and everyone kept forcing him to press the clit and aggravate the situation. Nice job."

"He threatened to come and burn the building down if he was hung up on again."

"And you hung up again."

"Yes. In hindsight not our finest hour. But the only option left was to tow the line and follow the guidelines set by management."

"By you?"

"Partially yes, I do not tolerate anyone using that type of language to my employees. So he was disconnected. How were we supposed to know he was a local man? That the pain and rage would actually lead him to come here and make good on his threat? It was a mistake, a costly mistake. He came in here and burned down most of the building."

"Were you here at the time?"

"Damn it all, yes. I was the one that gave the order to hang up. I caused it. The fire that killed fifteen employees was because of my hubris."

"That is insanity. Why didn't they have him go to the hospital? Get medical help?"

"Do you realize what that would have done to our stock? The bad press? Our board would have had me crucified for an incident like this."

"This wasn't the first time was it?"

"No. A bad batch of switches had come in from China. But a delay in production would have caused us to miss our goals for the quarter."

"So instead you let faulty equipment go out the door."

"Again, there were only three cases at that point in time. It was an acceptable failure rate. It was an astronomical chance it would occur, compounded with worldwide sales. It should have never occurred."

"How many times did it happen?"

"There have been less than a thousand cases. Out of millions of sales, an insignificant number."

"So many people suffered to make sales numbers."

"Less than half lost their genitals. We settled out and kept it under wraps. Mark, understand we are a global force for good. We feed starving children. Sponsor cleft palate surgeries in impoverished countries. A few hundred smashed cocks does not take away from that. We did no wrong."

"That is fucking terrible. You guys are disgusting."

"Mark, it is always easy to pass judgement from afar. You do not see the big picture. Give us a chance, join our team and see the Plastivag way."

"No thank you Richard. You disgust me, it actually makes me sick that you can justify your actions to turn a dollar. And now, history repeats itself and you still look down from your perch and try and explain it all away."

"Typical small minded fool. Fine. Fuck off and take your free 4000 and never return once this is all over."

"Keep your dick destroyer. I want nothing else from this place."

I want to sex you up

"This is Richard. Great. I will be right there. Good work. Any casualties? Acceptable. I will go to legal immediately. No, thank you. Be down soon. Mark, our time in this personal hell is done. I would say I enjoyed it, but frankly you are the exact type of person I feel sorry just being around. If we never meet again it will be too soon."

"Eat a bag of dicks."

"You as well."

Tonight on Vice News, an exclusive undercover expose on the world of sex toys and the lengths in which they will go to make a buck.

Watch our intrepid journalist go through the interview process at Plastivag Inc., a company known for putting on a happy public face. Home to the largest Christian care help center in North America. A company known for innovations and robotic sex partners, that hides a dark side.

Mark not only learned the truth of the fire that consumed their headquarters nearly seven years ago, but the darker secrets behind it. A tale of shady business practices and ruined lives; in a stunning turn of events that nearly replayed the tragic events of the past but may have also blown open the doors on the true man behind the Jack the Ripper and Dr H H Holmes killing streaks of the late 19th Century.

"This is Mark, eight months ago I went undercover to learn more about this secretive company. Since then I have uncovered a slew of secrets, mysteries and horrifying truths about the world leading sex device provider. A murky journey into the depths of sex and murder."

Tune in tonight and witness history, only on Vice News.